Anonymous

Daring Adventures among the Indians

Being a Narrative of Border Warfare and the Exploits of Famous Hunters

Anonymous

Daring Adventures among the Indians
Being a Narrative of Border Warfare and the Exploits of Famous Hunters

ISBN/EAN: 9783337336912

Printed in Europe, USA, Canada, Australia, Japan

Cover: Foto ©Andreas Hilbeck / pixelio.de

More available books at **www.hansebooks.com**

AMONG THE

INDIANS,

BEING

A Narrative of Border Warfare,

AND THE

EXPLOITS OF FAMOUS HUNTERS

———•••—

NEW YORK:

JOHN W. LOVELL COMPANY,

142 to 150 Worth St.; Mission Place.

MR. BRUCE DISCOVERING THE SOURCE OF THE NILE.

THRILLING ADVENTURES

OF

HUNTERS AND TRAVELLERS.

Discovery of the Source of the Nile.

THIS great discovery was effected in the year 1768, by James Bruce, a Scotch gentleman of education and fortune, and a most indefatigable traveller. After various travels and adventures in the north of Africa, and west of Asia, he determined to discover the

(7)

source of the Nile, of which the situation had been previously unknown to the civilized world. He formed the design while lying sick of a fever, at Aleppo.

On his recovery, he left that place for Alexandria, where he arrived on the 20th of June, 1768. From hence he proceeded by land to Rosetta, where he embarked on the Nile for Cairo.

After impressing the bey of the city with an idea of his skill in medicine and prophecy, he sailed to Syene, visiting in his way thither, the ruins of Thebes; and, on the 16th of February, 1769, set out from Kenne, through the Thebaid desert, to Corscir, on the Red Sea; and from thence proceeded to Tor and Jidda, where he landed on the 5th of May. After making several excursions in Arabia Felix, he quitted Loheia, on the 3d of September for Masuah; where, on his arrival, he was detained for some weeks, by the treachery and avarice of the governor of that place, who attempted to murder him, in consequence of his refusal to make him an enormous present. In February, 1770, he entered Gondar, the capital of Abyssinia, the ras of which city appointed him gentleman-usher of the king's bed-chamber, commander of the household cavalry, and governor of a province.

On the 27th of October, after having taken an active part in the councils of the the sovereign, and effected several cures of persons about the court attacked with the small-pox, he left the capital and set out in search of the source of the Nile, which he discovered at Saccala, on the 14th of the following November. The joy he felt on this occasion, is thus described by himself: "It is easier to guess, than to describe the situation of my mind at that moment; standing on that spot which had baffled the genius, history, and inquiry of both ancients and moderns, for the course of nearly three thousand years. Kings had attempted this discovery at the head of armies, and each expedition was distinguished from the last only by the difference of the numbers which had perished, and agreed alone in the dis-appointment which had uniformly, and without exception, followed them all. Fame, riches, and honor, had been held out, for a series of ages, to every individual of the myriads those princes commanded, without having produced one man capable of gratifying the curiosity of his sovereign, or wiping off the stain upon the enterprize and abilities of mankind, or adding this desideratum for the encouragement of geography. Though a mere private Briton, I triumphed here in my own mind over kings and their armies; and every comparison was leading nearer and nearer to the presumption, when the place itself where I stood, the object of my vain-glory, suggested what depressed my short-lived triumphs. I was but a few minutes arrived at the source of the Nile, through numberless dangers and sufferings, the least of which would have overwhelmed me, but for the continual goodness and and protection of Providence; I was, however, then but half through my journey, and all those dangers which I had already passed, awaited me again on my return. I found despondency gaining ground fast upon me, and blasting the crown of laurels I had rashly woven for myself."

After returning to Gondar, our traveller found much difficuly in obtaining permission to proceed on his way homeward; it being a rule with the inhabitants never to allow a stranger to quit Abyssinia. A civil war breaking out in the country about the period of his intended departure, he was compelled to remain in it till December of the following year, and took part in one of their battles, in which his valiant conduct was such that the king presented him with a rich suit of apparel, and a gold chain of immense value. At length, at the end of 1771, he set out from Gondar, and, in the February of the following year, arrived at Senaar, where he remained two months, suffering under the most inhospitable treatment, and deceived in his supplies of money, which compelled him to sell the gold chain he had been presented with. He then proceeded by Chiendi, and Gooz, through the Nubian desert, and on the 29th of November, reached Assouan, on the Nile, after a most dreadful and dangerous journey, in the course of which he lost all his camels and baggage, and twice laid himself down, in the expectation of death. Having procured, however, fresh camels, he returned to the desert, and recovered most part of his baggage, with which, on the 10th of January, he arrived at Cairo; where, ingratiating himself with the bey, he obtained permission for English commanders to bring their vessels and merchandize to Suez, as well as to Jidda, an advantage no other European nation had before been able to acquire.

In the beginning of March he arrived at Alexandria, whence he sailed to Marseilles; where he landed about the end of the month, suffering under great agony from a disease called the Guinea worm, which totally disabled him from walking, and had nearly proved fatal to him during his voyage. Notwithstanding, however, the perils he underwent, and the barbarities he witnessed in the course of his travels, and particularly at Abyssinia, yet even that country he left

with some regret, and would often recall,
with a feeling of tenderness, the kindnesses
he had received there, especially from the
ras's wife, Ozoro Esther, between himself
and whom, a very affectionate intimacy had
existed.

Fatal Adventure in Australia.

THE great island of Australia is claimed by the British government, which has a colony, called New South Wales, upon its southern coast. Many attempts have been made by bold traders to explore the interior of the island, but as yet, very little is known about it. Major Mitchell was engaged about seven months in exploring the wild country north-west of New South Wales. He encountered many dangers and endured many hardships. Among his party was a gentle-

(14)

A NATIVE OF AUSTRALIA.

man named Richard Cunningham, who was
a botanist. While in pursuit of his favorite
study he met a most awful fate.

On the 17th of April, at the close of a
very hot day, it was reported that Mr. Cunningham was missing.   At first his absence
did not create much uneasiness.   But as
the night passed, and nothing was heard
of him, Major Mitchell was fearful that he
would perish for want of water, in the arid
region, which he was traversing.   Two parties started in search of the missing botanist.   But they sought in vain.   Upon the
23d, two whites came into the camp, and
reported that they had found the track of
Mr. Cunningham's horse, and had followed it
for many miles, until it entered a thicket,
and was lost.   The humane major immediately set out in the direction it was supposed Mr. Cunningham would take.   For
several days the search was continued.
Every device was resorted to, to guide the
unfortunate man to the camp, if he was still
alive.   All was fruitless.   His friends remained uncertain of his fate.

B   2*

At length, the mystery was solved. A party sent for the express purpose to the Bogan country, in October, 1835, captured a band of forty natives, men, women, and children, who gave up three men of their tribe, as the *murderers* of Mr. Cunningham. A knife, a glove, and a cigar-case, belonging to that gentleman, were found in the bags of the tribe. The three murderers confessed the deed.

Cunningham had come up to them on the Bogan one evening, and made signs for food. They gave it to him, and he encamped with them that night. The botanist got up repeatedly in the night, and this, said the natives, excited their suspicions, and they resolved to destroy him, which they effected by coming behind him, and striking him with a heavy weapon on the head. The truth of this confession was made evident, by the natives taking the party to the spot, and showing them poor Cunningham's bleaching bones. They were gathered up, laid in the earth, and a humble mound erected over them. Unfortunately, two of the murderers escaped from their captors, and only one was brought down to the white settlements to pay for his crime. A fourth man had been present at the murder, but he never fell into the hands of the white party.

The Sailor and the Bear.

A HULL whaler was moored to a field of
ice, on which, at a considerable distance, a
large bear was observed prowling about for
prey. One of the ship's company, embold-
ened by an artificial courage—derived from
the free use of his rum, which in his econo-
my he had stored for special occasions—
(20)

SCENE IN THE ARTIC REGIONS.

undertook to pursue and attack the bear that was within view. Armed only with a whale-lance, he resolutely, and against all persuasion, set out on his adventurous exploit. A fatiguing journey of about half a league, over a surface of yielding snow and rugged hammocks, brought him within a few yards of the enemy, which to his surprise, undauntedly faced him, and seemed to invite him to the combat.

His courage being, by this time, greatly subdued, partly by the evaporation of the stimulus he had employed, and partly by the undismayed and even threatening aspect of the bear, he levelled his lance in an attitude suited either to offensive or defensive action, and stopped. The bear also stood still. In vain the adventurer tried to rally courage to make the attack; his enemy was too formidable, and his appearance too imposing. In vain also he shouted, advanced his lance, and made feints of attack; the enemy, either not understanding them, or despising such unmanliness, obstinately stood his ground. Already the limbs of

the sailor began to snake, the lance trembled in the rest, and his gaze, which had
hither been steadfast, began to quiver; but
the fear of ridicule from his messmates still
had its influence, and he yet scarcely dared
to retreat.

Bruin, however, possessing less reflection,
or being more regardless of consequences,
began, with the most audacious boldness,
to advance. His near approach, and un-
shaken step subdued the spark of bravery
and dread of ridicule that had hitherto up-
held our adventurer; he turned and fled.
But now was the time of danger. The
sailor's flight encouraged the bear in his
turn to pursue; and being better practised
in snow travelling, and better provided for
it, he rapidly gained upon the fugitive. The
whale-lance, his only defence encumbered
him in his retreat, he threw it down and
kept on. This fortunately excited the bear's
attention; he stopped, pawed it, bit it, and
then resumed the chace. Again he was at
the heels of the panting seaman, who, conscious of the favorable effect of the lance,

dropped a mitten; the stratagem succeeded, and while Bruin again stopped to examine it, the fugitive, improving the interval, made considerable progress ahead.

Still the bear resumed the pursuit, with the most provoking perseverance, excepting when arrested by another mitten, and finally by a hat, which he tore to shreds between his teeth and his paws, and would no doubt have soon made the incautious adventurer his victim, who was rapidly losing strength and heart, but for the prompt, and well-timed assistance of his shipmates, who, observing that the affair had assumed a dangerous aspect, sallied out to his rescue.

The little phalanx opened him a passage, and then closed to receive the bold assailant. Though now beyond the reach of his adversary, the dismayed fugitive continued onward, impelled by his fears, and never relaxed his exertions until he fairly reached the shelter of the ship.

Bruin once more prudently came to a stand, and for a moment seemed to survey his enemies with all the consideration of an experienced general; when, finding them too numerous for any reasonable hope of success, he very wisely wheeled about, and succeeded in making a safe and honorable retreat.

WOLVES ATTACKING A PARTY IN A SLEIGH.

Adbentures with Wolves.

WOLVES are still numerous in some parts of France, where they commit dreadful devastations. Even in the thickly inhabited districts, these ferocious animals are sometimes seen, and the people are forced to be on their guard.

A few winters ago, Monsieur de B., an advocate of Dijon, was returning rather late from a shooting excursion, near that town, when his dog, a small pointer, who was a few paces in advance, ran suddenly back, as if terrified.

The spot was a long hollow, formed by two sandbanks; and as far as his eye could reach, he could discover no cause for the animal's sudden terror, which sent him crouching to his feet. He proceeded cautiously, however, cocking both barrels of his gun; for upwards of two hundred yards no cause of alarm presented itself. Indeed. he had forgotten the circumstance, and rested the gun across his shoulder, when the dog again fell behind him with an affrightened yell. A wolf stood on the sandbank, about thirty yards before him.

Armed only with partridge shot, Monsieur de B. considered it most prudent to retreat, and gain a cross road in the rear. He had not returned many yards, when to his horror and astonishment, he beheld another wolf barring his path on that side.

Neither as yet had ventured to attack him, and as he advanced, each retired; but the other would draw closer to his heels. His situation became critical, for night was approaching, and he feared that with it more assailants would be down upon him; and to this they both howled as if to call a reinforcement, and the sportsman at length felt certain they were answered from the hills. No time was to be lost; he rapidly advanced on one, and within twenty paces fired both barrels at him. The wolf fell, wounded, and the other cleared the bank, Monsieur B., following his example, took to his heels, and never drew breath till he had entered Dijon.

On examining the snow the next morning, it was ascertained that he had been hotly pursued to the very gates. As for the wounded wolf, a few bones were all that his comrades had left of him.

The wolves of Russia are noted for their sagacity. In the thinly settled districts, they are very abundant. The public roads are rendered dangerous by the number and daring character of these fierce animals. Travellers are very often attacked, and if they are not well-armed, or near to some village, their destruction is certain.

One day some peasants were travelling, in a sleigh, when they were suddenly attacked by a large number of wolves. The house, at which they intended to stop, was about two miles from the place where they were attacked. They were without weapons of any kind, and their only hope was in flight. Keeping the wolves back as well as they could, they whipped the horses, and drove for the house with the utmost speed. The savage beasts pursued, occasionally jumping upon the sleigh, and snapping their greedy jaws as they ran by the side of the horses. The party reached the house. The gate of the yard happened to be closed. But the almost maddened horses dashed it open, and the party entered the yard. Nine wolves entered with them. Fortunately the gate swung shut, and the wolves were caught in a trap. From being the most ferocious of beasts, the nature of the animals, now that they found escape impossible, completely changed. So

WOLVES AND VULTURES FEASTING ON HUMAN REMAINS.

far, indeed, from attempting to molest any one, they slunk into holes, and allowed themselves to be slaughtered without resistance. This escape was miraculous.

The wolf shares with the vulture in feasting upon the bodies of those who are slain in battle, and left unburied on the field. Sometimes they will scratch away the earth, and tear the bodies from their rude graves. It is an awful sight to see these fierce animals making a meal at midnight upon human flesh and bones.

Remarkable Tiger Hunt.

THE following account of a tiger hunt in Java, is given by a sailor, in a letter to his brother, dated December 19th, 1832.

At seven o'clock, on the morning of October 2d, I set out with my two sons, a Berzoekie man in my service, and about fifty natives, armed with pikes and hog-spears; I was armed with a gun and a spear. The tiger for which we were on the look-out was in a valley about two miles and a half distant from our port. The moment we arrived near him we commenced operations. About nine o'clock we effectually drove him out of his den of under-wood; and while he was doubling the brow of a hill, I had a rap at him, which took effect. He now made over to the west side of the valley, and into a thorny bush. In half an hour we started him again; he then

(36)

THE TIGER.

ran along the western side of the valley into another bush: several spears were now thrown at him, but without effect.

We followed, and soon roused him again; he now made a start for his old station on the east side of the valley; he seemed to be very much fagged on account of the heat and a want of water, and it became difficult to arouse him; several spears flew after him, but they fell short. All this time, although pretty close, I could not get a shot at him, sometimes on account of my people, and at others not wishing to throw a shot away, not knowing how soon I might require it in self-defence. Close to his heels, we followed him across the valley.

He now took shelter in a bush on the side of a hill, where he remained growling for some time. He saw that he was in danger, so he made a start from that bush to another, just at my feet, and lay for at least ten minutes, not ten yards from where I was with one of my sons, who was making an opening into the bush, so that at length I got a clear sight of him; but before we could finish our task, he made a spring with an intention to clear the heads of three men who were to my right at about a fathom distance, but they received and put three pikes and a hogspear into him : the former entered his belly, the latter entered his right shoulder; this he took with him, but the pike staves all broke.

This shock to his frame brought him down on one of the men, on whom he left the marks of three of his paws, but he got into a bush before I could turn round to have a rap at him. This was his last move. It was now just twelve at noon. We gathered up our broken pike-staves, bound up the wounds of our man, and sent him off to the mill, to await our arrival; but determined not to give up our prize, we remained quiet for about an hour, to rest ourselves. During this time he growled once, but faintly; he was at that time drawing the hogspear out of his right shoulder. This gave him much pain, and made him growl. We now saw the bush shake very much, so again we began operations, by cutting down the small bushes to get a sight of him; this was soon done, and I put a shot into his head. Our work was now done, so we went up to him.

I had him carried home. His weight was three hundred and thirty-three pounds; he stood three feet three inches high; length of body six feet, tail two feet four inches. I then dressed the wounded hunter. He was fourteen days under my hands. He had ten wounds on his body, left arm and head. This, you will say is no children's play.

Escape of two boys from the Indians.

In the fall of the year 1793, two boys, named John and Henry Johnson, whose parents lived near Carpenter's station, on the east side of the Ohio river, were captured by two Indians, who lay in ambush near the house. After travelling nearly all day, the Indians halted, and kindled a fire.

When night came on the fire was covered up, the boys pinioned, and made to lie down together. The Indians then placed the hoppis straps over them, and lay down, one on each side of them, on the ends of the

AN INDIAN CHIEF.

straps. Pretty late in the night the Indians fell asleep; and one of them becoming cold, caught hold of John in his arms, and turned him over on the outside. In this situation, the boy, who had kept awake, found means to get his hands loose. He then whispered to his brother, made him get up, and untied his arms. This done, Henry thought of nothing but running off as fast as possible; but when about to start, John caught hold of him, saying, " We must kill these Indians before we go." After some hesitation, Henry agreed to make the attempt. John then took one of the rifles of the Indians, and placed it on a log, with the muzzle close to the head of one of them. He then cocked the gun, and placed his little brother at the breech, with his finger on the trigger, with instructions to pull it as soon as he should strike the other Indian.

He then took one of the Indian's tomahawks, and, standing astride of the other Indian, struck him with it. The blow, however fell on the back of the neck and to one side, so as not to be fatal. The Indian then attempted to spring up, but the little fellow repeated the blow with such force and rapidity on the skull, that, as he expressed it, "the Indian lay still and began to quiver."

At the moment of the first stroke given by the elder brother with the tomahawk, the younger one pulled the trigger, and shot away a considerable portion of the Indian's lower jaw. This Indian, a moment after receiving the shot, began to flounce about and yell in the most frightful manner. The boys then made the best of their way to the fort, and reached it a little before daybreak. On getting near the fort they found the people all up and in great agitation on their account. On hearing a woman exclaim, "Poor little fellows they are killed or taken prisoners!" the oldest one answered, "No, mother, we are here yet."

Having brought nothing away with them from the Indian camp, their relation of what had taken place between them and the Indians was not fully credited. A small party was soon made up to go and ascertain the truth or falsehood of their report.

On arriving at the place they found the Indian whom the oldest brother had tomahawked, lying dead in the camp: the other had crawled away, and taken his gun and shot-pouch with him. After scalping the Indian, the party returned to the fort; and the same day a larger party went out to look after the wounded Indian, who had crawled some distance from the camp, and concealed himself in the top of a fallen tree, where, notwithstanding the severity of the wound, he determined to sell his life as dearly as possible.

Having fixed his gun for the purpose, on the approach of the men to a proper distance, he took aim at one of them, and pulled the trigger, but his gun missed fire. The party, concluding that the Indian would die at any rate, thought best to retreat, and return and look for him after some time. On returning, however, he could not be found, having crawled away and concealed himself in some other place. His skeleton and gun were found some time afterwards.

Capture of Mr. Moore's Family.

MR. MOORE resided in the north-western part of Virginia, which was frequently over-run by parties of Indians from the Shawnese towns.

On the 14th of July, 1786, early in the morning, a gang of horses had come in from the lick-blocks, about one hundred yards from the house, and Mr. Moore had gone out to salt them. Two men also, who were living with him, had gone out, and were reaping wheat. The Indians, about thirty

(18)

POLLY HIDING BEHIND THE BARRELS.

D   5

in number, who were lying in ambush, watching the house, supposing that all the men were absent, availed themselves of the opportunity, and rushed forward with all speed. As they advanced they commenced firing, and killed three of the children, viz. William and Rebecca, who were returning from the spring, and Alexander in the yard.

Mr. Moore attempted to get to the house, but finding it surrounded, ran past it through a small pasture in which the house stood. When he reached the fence he made a halt, and was shot through with seven bullets. The Indians said he might have escaped if he had not stopped on the fence. After he was shot he ran about forty yards, and fell. He was then scalped by the Indians, and afterwards buried by the whites at the place where the body lay, and where his grave may yet be seen. It was thought that when he saw his family about to be massacred, without the possibility of rendering them any assistance, he chose to share a like fate.

There were two fierce dogs, which fought

like heroes until the fiercest one was killed. The two men who were reaping, hearing the alarm and seeing the house surrounded, fled, and alarmed the settlement.   At that time the nearest family was six miles distant. As soon as the alarm was given, Mrs. Moore and Miss Martha Ivins, who was living in the family, helping them to spin, barred the door, but this was of no avail. There was no man in the house except John Simpson, an old Englishman, and he was on the loft sick, and in bed.   There were five or six guns in the house, but having been shot off the evening before, they where then empty.   It was intended to have loaded them after breakfast. Martha Ivins took two of them and went up stairs were Simpson was, and, handing them to him, told him to shoot.   He looked up, but had been shot in the head through a crack, and was then near his end.

Martha then went to a far end of the house, lifted up a loose plank, and went under the floor. Polly Moore, a child of about eight years, hid behind some barrels in the loft. In the meantime, the Indians cut down the door, and entered the house. Mrs. Moore and her children, John, Jane, Peggy, and were soon secured. An Indian then went up into the loft, where he found Polly, almost frightened to death, huddled behind the barrels.

The Indians then left the house, with their prisoners; and Martha, thinking they had gone away entirely, came from her hiding-place, ran out and got behind a log, not far from the house. The Indians were still about, trying to catch the horses, and preparing to set the dwelling and out-houses on fire. Martha believing that one of them saw her behind the log, got up and ran to-towards a small building, near the dwelling, used as a tool-house. As she reached the door, an Indian threw his tomahawk at her. The weapon buried itself in the door, near Martha's head, and she was uninjured. She then reflected that escape was impossible, and gave herself up, at which the Indian seemed very much pleased. The houses were then set on fire.

The whole party then set out for the Indian towns. Perceiving that John Moore was a boy, weak in body and mind, and unable to travel, they killed him the first day. The babe, Margaret, they took two or three days, but it being fretful, on account of a wound it had received, they dashed its brains out against a tree. They then moved on with haste to their towns. For some time it was usual to tie very securely each of the prisoners at night, and for a warrior to lie beside each of them with tomahawk in hand, so that in case of pursuit, the prisoners might be speedily dispatched.

Not unfrequently they were several days without food, and when they killed game, their habit was to make broth. When they reach their town, they were soon assembled in council, when an old man made a long speech to them dissuading them from war; but at the close of it the warriors shook their heads and retired. The old man afterwards took Polly Moore into his family, where he and his wife seemed greatly to commiserate her situation, and showed all

MARTHA'S ESCAPE TO THE TOOL-HOUSE.

possible kindness.   Shortly after they arrived at the towns, Mrs. Moore and her daughter Jane were put to death, being burned at the stake.   This lasted some time, during which she manifested the utmost Christian fortitude, and bore it without a murmur—at intervals conversing with her daughter, Polly, and Martha Ivins, and expressing great anxiety for the moment to arrive when her soul should wing its way to the bosom of her Saviour.   At length an old squaw, more humane than the rest, dispatched her with a tomahawk.

This tribe of Indians proving very troublesome to the whites, it was repeatedly contemplated to send an expedition to their town.   This it is probable, Martha Ivins in some measure postponed, by sending communications through the traders, urging the probable fate of the prisoners, if it were done immediately. In November, two years afterwards, however, such an expedition did go out.   The Indians were aware of it from about the time it started, and when it drew near they concealed what they could not carry off, and, with the prisoners, left their towns. About this time Polly Moore had serious thoughts of concealing herself until the arrival of the whites; but fearing the consequences of a greater delay in their arrival than she might anticipate, she did not attempt it.

Late in November, however, the expedition did arrive, and after having burned their towns, destroyed their corn, &c., returned home. After this the Indians returned to their towns; but winter having set in, and finding themselves without houses or food, they were greatly dispirited, and went to Detroit, where, giving themselves up to great excess in drinking, they sold Polly Moore to a man living in or near a little village named French Town, near the western end of Lake Erie, for half a gallon of rum. Though at this time the winter was very severe, the released captive had nothing to protect her feet but a pair of deerskin moccasins.

Martha Ivins, and Polly and Peggy Moore, were ransomed some months after this time.

They displayed much fortitude amid the dreadful suffering they were compelled to undergo, yet it was very long before they could shake off the remembrance of the horrible fate of the other members of their family.

Rescue of Catharine Gunn.

In 1764, a party of about fifty Indians entered the northern part of Virginia, and then dividing into two, one went towards the Roanoke and Catawba settlements, and the other in the direction of Jackson's river, where each committed murders and depredations. Captain Paul was then in command of the garrison of Fort Dinwiddie. Hearing of the depredations of the Indians who visited Jackson's river, he went in pur-

THE MASSACRE.

suit of them. After a long and rapid march, in the direction it was supposed the red men had taken, the captain accidentally came upon them at midnight, as they were encamped on New River, at the mouth of Indian creek.

The whites delivered their fire, and then rushed in upon the startled foe. The struggle was short. Most of the Indians fled, or were killed or captured. One of them went up to a woman, who sat composed upon the ground, and was about to strike his tomahawk into her head, when a bold ranger rushed between and took the Indian by the throat. He was about to draw his knife and stab him, when Captain Paul interfered and took the man from him. Paul was ever anxious to save life. He never slew when he could capture. Another one of his men was about to strike his tomahawk into the head of the supposed squaw, when the captain threw himself between, and received the blow upon his arm. "It's a shame to hurt a woman, even a squaw." She proved to be Mrs. Catharine Gunn, an

English woman, an acquaintance of Captain Paul, made prisoner on the Catawba a few days before, when her husband and two children were killed.

The captain asked her why she did not make known that she was a prisoner, by crying out. The poor woman replied: "I had as soon be killed as not—my husband is murdered—my children are slain—my parents are dead. I have not a relation in America—every thing dear to me is gone; I have no wishes, no hopes, no fears—I would not have risen to my feet to have saved my life." These words are the simple expression of utter despair—of a spirit dead to the world before its time had come to seek another sphere. Having punished the savages for their atrocities, Captain Paul returned to Fort Dinwiddie.

POE'S FIGHT WITH TWO INDIANS.

Adam Poe's Fight with two Indians.

About the middle of July, 1782, seven Wyandotts crossed the Ohio a few miles above Wheeling, and committed great depredations upon the southern shore, killing an old man whom they found alone in his cabin, and spreading terror throughout the neighborhood. Within a few hours after their retreat, eight men assembled from different parts of the small settlement, and

(67)

pursued the enemy with great expedition. Among the most active and efficient of the party, were two brothers, Adam and Andrew Poe. They had not followed the trail far, before they became satisfied that the depredators were conducted by Big Foot, a renowned chief of the Wyandott tribe, who derived his name from the immense size of his feet.

Adam Poe was overjoyed at the idea of measuring his strength with that of so celebrated a chief, and urged the pursuit with a keenness that soon brought him in the vicinity of the enemy. For the last few miles, the trail had led them up the southern bank of the Ohio, where the footprints in the sand were deep and obvious, but when within a few hundred yards of the point at which the whites as well as the Indians were in the habit of crossing, it suddenly diverged from the stream, and stretched along a rocky ridge. Here Adam halted, for a moment, and directed his brother and the other young men to follow the trail with proper caution, while he himself still adhered to the river path, which led through a cluster of willows directly to the point where he supposed the enemy to lie. Having examined the priming of his gun, he crept cautiously through the bushes, until he had a view of the point of embarkation. Here lay two canoes, showing that the Indians were close at hand, he relaxed nothing of his vigilance, and gaining a jutting cliff, which hung immediately over the canoes, he peered cautiously over, and beheld the object of his search.

The gigantic Big Foot, lay below him in the shade of a willow, and was talking in a low deep tone to another warrior, who seemed a mere pigmy by his side. Adam cautiously drew back and cocked his gun. The mark was fair—the distance did not exceed twenty feet, and his aim was unerring. Raising his rifle slowly and cautiously, he took a steady aim at Big Foot's breast, and drew the trigger. His gun flashed. Both Indians sprung to their feet with a deep interjection of surprise. Adam was too much hampered by the bushes to retreat, and setting his life upon a cast of the die, he sprung over the bush which had sheltered him, and summoning all his powers, leaped boldly down the precipice upon the breast of Big Foot with a shock that bore him to the earth.

At the moment of contact, Adam had thrown his right arm around the neck of the smaller Indian, so that all three came to the earth at once. At that moment a sharp firing was heard among the bushes above, announcing that the other parties were engaged, but the trio below were too busy to attend to any thing but themselves. Big Foot was for an instant stunned by the violence of the shock, and Adam was enabled to keep them both down. But the exertion necessary for that purpose was so great, that he had no leisure to use his knife. Big Foot quickly recovered, and without attempting to rise, wrapped his long arms around Adam's body, and pressed him to his breast with the crushing force of a boa constrictor.

Adam instantly relaxed his hold of the

small Indian, who sprung to his feet.   Big
Foot then ordered him to run for his tomahawk, which lay within ten steps, and kill
the white man while he held him in his
arms.   Adam, seeing his danger,   struggled
manfully to extricate himself from the folds
of the giant, but in vain.   The lesser Indian approached with his uplifted tomahawk, but Adam watched him closely, and
as he was about to strike, gave him a kick
so sudden and violent, as to knock the tomahawk out of his hand, and send him stag-
gering back into the water.   But the lesser
Indian again approached, carefully avoiding
Adam's heels, and making many motions
with his tomahawk, in order to deceive him
as to the point where the blow would fall.

Such was Adam's dexterity and vigilance,
however, that he managed to receive the
tomahawk in a glancing direction upon the
left wrist, wounding him deeply, but not
disabling him. He now made a sudden and
desperate effort to free himself from the
arms of the giant, and succeeded. Instantly
snatching up a rifle, for the Indian could

not venture to shoot for fear of hurting his companion, he shot the lesser Indian through the body. But scarcely had he done so, when Big Foot arose, and placing one hand upon his collar, and the other upon his hip, pitched him into the air, as he himself would have pitched a child.

Adam fell upon his back at the edge of the water, but before his antagonist could spring upon him, he was again upon his feet, and stung with rage at the idea of being handled so easily, he attacked his gigantic antagonist with a fury which for a time compensated for inferiority of strength. It was now a fair fist fight between them, for in the hurry of the struggle neither had leisure to draw their knives. Adam's superior activity and experience as a pugilist, gave him great advantage. The Indian struck awkwardly, and finding himself rapidly dropping to leeward, he closed with his antagonist, and again hurled him to the ground. They quickly rolled into the river, and the struggle continued with unabated fury, each attempting to drown the other.

The Indian being unused to such violent exertion, and having been much injured by the first shock in his stomach, was unable to exert the same powers which had given him such a superiority at first; and Adam, seizing him by the scalp-lock, put his head under water, and held it there until the faint struggles of the Indian induced him to believe that he was drowned, when he relaxed his hold and attempted to draw his knife. The Indian, however, instantly regained his feet, and in his turn put his adversary under.

In the struggle, both were carried out in the current beyond their depth, and each was compelled to relax his hold and swim for his life. There was still one loaded rifle upon the shore, and each swam hard in order to reach it, but the Indian proved the most expert swimmer, and Adam seeing that he should be too late, turned and swam out into the stream, intending to dive, and thus frustrate his enemy's intention.

At this instant, Andrew, having heard that his brother was alone in a struggle with two Indians, and in great danger, ran up hastily to the bank above, in order to assist him. Another white man followed him closely, and seeing Adam in the river, covered with blood, and swimming rapidly from shore, mistook him for an Indian and fired upon him, wounding him dangerously in the shoulder.

Adam turned, and seeing his brother, called loudly upon him "to shoot the big Indian upon shore." Andrew's gun, however, was empty, having just been discharged. Fortunately, Big Foot had also seized the gun with which Adam had shot the Indian, so that both were upon equality. The contest was now who should load first. Fig Foot poured in his powder first, and drawing his ramrod out of its sheath in too great a hurry, threw it into the river, and while he ran to recover it, Andrew gained an advantage. Still the Indian was but a second too late, for his gun was at his shoulder, when Andrew's ball entered his breast. The gun dropped from his hands and he fell forward upon his face upon the very margin of the river. Andrew, now alarmed for his brother, who was scarcely able to swim, threw down his gun and rushed into the river and brought him ashore. Adam Poe recovered of his wounds, and lived many years after his conflict; but never forgot the tremendous *hug* which he sustained in the arms of Big Foot.

Adventures in Mexico.

MEXICO is a very interesting country. The manners, customs, and institutions of the people are very different from those of the people of the United States. Since the war between the two great republics, many travellers from the States have visited Mexico, to see its grand and beautiful scenery, and to gain a knowledge of the condition of the people. Some of their adventures are amusing and instructive. The means of travelling

(76)

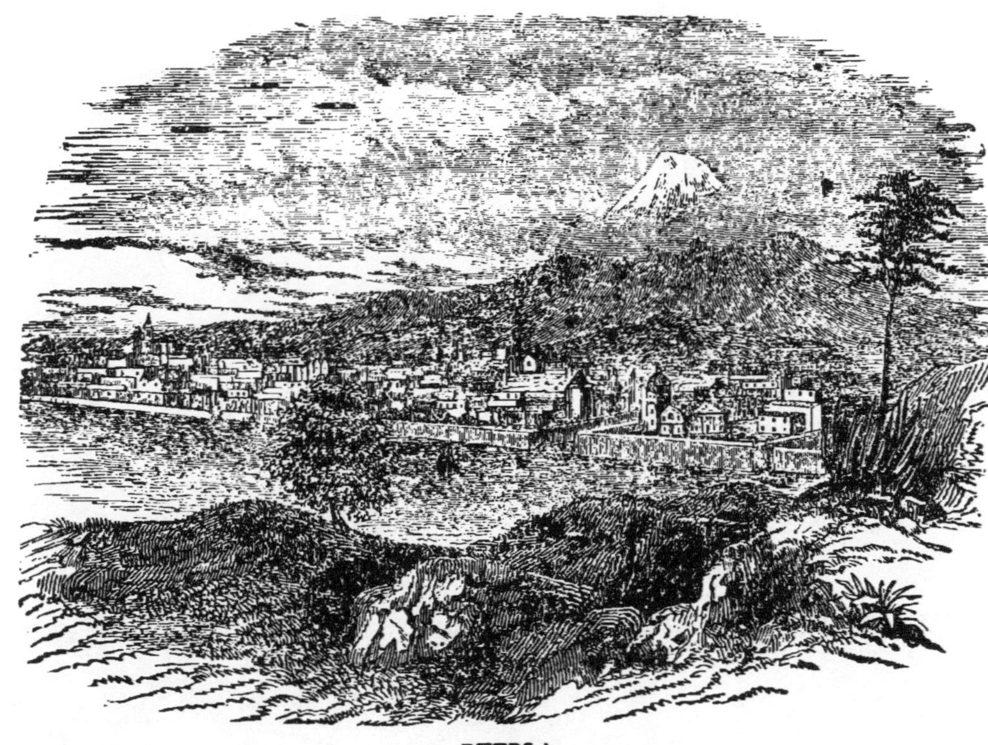

PUEBLA.

are very defective, and nearly all the roads are infested with brigands, who do not scruple to murder, if that is necessary to obtain plunder.

Not long ago a traveller was proceeding along the great road, which leads from the city of Vera Cruz to the capital. He rode upon a mule, and was attended by two Mexicans, also upon mules. The natives had assured the traveller that there was no danger of the brigands attacking him— that the troops had routed them, and broken up their strongest band. Under the guidance of these men, the traveller proceeded, in the full confidence of safety. But it seems that the guides were brigands themselves, who had offered their services, for the purpose of lulling the suspicions of the gentleman. Not many miles from Puebla de los Angelos, one of the largest cities in Mexico, the road wound through a deep ravine, upon each side of which were dense thickets. One of the guides suddenly gave a signal, by a shrill whistle, when the traveller found himself surrounded.

BANDITS PLUNDERING.

All thought of defence was useless. Twenty pieces were at once leveled at him. He made signs of submission, and the pieces were lowered. As quick as thought, the baggage was removed from the mules, and ransacked. The traveller had much that was valuable—a large sum of money, fine clothes, and some jewelry. The robbers took all that promised to be of the least use to them. When the traveller attempted to remonstrate, they pointed their weapons at him, and intimated that he was fortunate to escape with his life. They even

CITY OF MEXICO.

stripped the fine coat from his back. Then, having collected the plunder, they mounted it upon the mules, and ordered some of the party to drive them swiftly in one direction, while they took a by-path through the thicket. The traveller was then forced to walk to Puebla, stripped of all that he had brought with to pay his way. In that city, he told his tale, and found kind friends among the priests, one of whom took him into his house to live, until he could write home to his family in the United States, to send him money. He was but one of many sufferers from the attacks of the brigands.

The city of Mexico is beautifully situated in a valley, almost surrounded by lofty mountains. Its buildings are generally of a substantial and elegant construction. The inhabitants are lively, intelligent, and fond of pleasure. The great square, or " Plaza," is thronged at evening, with promenaders and pleasure-seekers. Upon one side of this square is the National Palace, a splendid edifice, where the members of the government hold their meetings.

The great celebration of the Carnival is one of the most remarkable features of Mexican life. Mr. W. W. Carpenter, thus narrates what he saw of this festival: "The Mexicans go round at night, breaking egg-shells on the heads of persons. These are filled with flour, and scented with Cologne, or rose water, or some other rich odor. When it commenced I was standing in the the street, idling away the time as best I could, when, all of a sudden, my hat was removed, and a number of these odious shells were broken on my devoted head. Not being aware of the custom, I quickly turned, and, before I was aware of it, had knocked down the man who was guilty of what I considered this insult. A tumult was raised; they threatened to kill me, and perhaps would have done so, had not some one gone after the alcalde. He came and inquired into the matter, then ordered them to let me alone for the future, and took me back to his house. Were it not for my friend, Don Jesus Murguir, and the alcalde, I fear I would not have been long in this world; but when I was in difficulty, right or wrong, I was sure of their protection.

This diversion is practised several nights in succession, varied occasionally by throwing flour in person's faces. It is followed by the religious season of Lent, which continues forty days; and it is the custom throughout Mexico to have mass, or at least religious service, every morning during all that time. When the festival commenced, the people assembled as usual in the morning. When they came out of the church, I noticed, with curiosity, that all the people had a cross painted upon their foreheads. For what purpose this was done I could not ascertain. This they wore for one week; and then commenced the processions.

One morning I resolved to observe one of these closely, to see all that could be seen. The procession formed in the suburbs of the town, so thither I went. On coming up, I saw the priest mounting a donkey, richly comparisoned, and led by two boys. The streets were strewed with flowers, evergreens, and the finest blankets. This, I suppose, was intended to represent the entry of Christ into Jerusalem.

They were attended with music, banners were flying, and rockets were fired. They went through the principal streets, then turned up to the church; but as they were going through the Plaza, some other donkeys commenced braying, when the one that was rode by the representative of Christ answered it, and started off, notwithstanding the exertions of the boys to prevent him. When he found he had some difficulty in getting away, he began to kick and plunge, and, finally, he threw his priestship off. This scene was so comical and ridiculous, that, had it broken his neck, 1 could not have avoided smiling, and laughing when I had a better chance. Not so with them, however, for not a smile could be seen on a single face. People were coming from all parts of the country to witness the ceremonies and to confess, this being the time for a general confession.

An Arab Tournament.

SIR GEORGE TEMPLE, an English traveller who spent some time among the Arabs, thus describes one of their tournaments, such as he frequently witnessed: The tournament field is oblong, and bordered by rows of spectators, who form its boundaries, by sitting cross-legged round the open space.

(87)

The best riders of the tribe, mounted on
the most active horses, are then introduced
into the arena, the men being clothed with
as much splendor as their means will permit them, while the chargers are covered
with large silk housings of different colors,
reaching to the ground, and resembling
those of ancient knights, as represented ir
Froissart.

Some of the Arabs then commence making their horses dance to the sound of drums
and trumpets, whilst men on foot occasionally rush forward and discharge their mus-
ketry close to the horses' ears. Others dash
forward at full speed along the line of seated
spectators, as close to their feet as they
possibly can, without actually trampling on
them: and every now and then suddenly
throw their horses on their haunches, spin
them round on their hind legs, and resume
in the opposite direction their wild career.

It is a nervous sight to behold; for you
momentarily expect to see some person or
child crushed beneath the horses' hoofs;
but no accident ever happens, and men,

women, and children, maintain their seats with the greatest calmness and feeling of security, saluting any well-executed point of horsemanship with loud and exulting shouts of approbation, whilst the women accompany them with the usual but indescribable cries of the quick-repeated lu-lu-lu-lu; in return for which they are covered with clouds of sand and dust, which the impetuous coursers throw up behind them.

Three or four others, dashing their sharp stirrups into the flanks of their impatient steeds, rush madly along the length of the arena, shouting forth their *tekbir*, or war-cries, and whirling round their heads the long and silver adorned Arab guns, which they discharge at the spectators when they have reached the farthest extremity of the lists.

Others engage with swords soldiers on foot, galloping round their adversaries in incredibly small circles, twisting their horses suddenly round, and then circling to the other hand; and I know not which most to admire, the activity and suppleness of the rider, or of his horse. Others, whilst at full speed, will lean over, and without in the least reducing their pace, pick up from the ground a piastre or any other equally small object, thrown for the purpose.

These sports form on the whole one of gayest and most animated scenes I ever beheld, increased as it is by the waving of many silken sanjaks of the brightest colors, by the music, and the report of fire-arms, the war-cries of the performers, and the shouts of the spectators.

An Adventure in Italy.

The following account of a singular display of ferocity, by a herd of swine in Italy,
is given by an English tourist: I will tell
you of a narrow escape I had some years
ago, in Tuscany. R— and myself having
heard of a flight of cocks, had gone down
into the Maremma to shoot. You have
heard of the Maremma. It possesses an
almost interminable extent of morasses,
"overgrown with long, rank grasses," a
wilderness of putridity and desolation. It
was the month of November; before which
time it is dangerous to set foot there, for
until the first frost even many of the fever-
stricken serfs forsake it. In the eagerness
of sport we had been led farther than we
calculated from our albergo, a solitary,
wretched hovel, bordering on the marsh,
the abode of the most ghostly, yellow, ema-

ciated objects in human form I ever beheld, except some of the cayenned, curry-dried, liver-worn Anglo-East Indians we left at Cheltenham. The sun was fast setting, and we had still two miles to make, and were coasting along the edge of a knoll, thickly set with huge and speckled aloes, intermingled here and there with stunted ilexes, and with the strawberry tree, then bright with its globes of deep red gold, when methought I heard a rustling among the branches, and a sound like that of the grinding of teeth. I noticed it to my companion. He suddenly turned ashy-pale, and whispered hysterically, "We are near a herd of swine."

Vast numbers, I should have told you, are turned out in the fall of the leaf, to fatten here, and become so savage and wild, that none but their keepers dare approach them, and cased as they are in an almost impenetrable mail of leather, even they sometimes fall victims to the ferocity of these brutes.

"It is well for us," continued my friend "that there is a hut within a few hundred yards. Let us lose no time in making for it." As he spake, the sounds became louder, and I saw some hundred hogs emerging from the brushwood, grunting fiercely, and gnashing their teeth in unison. They were huge, gaunt, long-legged, long-headed, and long-backed creatures, giants of their species—spectral monsters, more like starved bloodhounds than swine.

They now mustered their forces in battle array, outside the thicket, and commenced the attack in a systematic and regularly concerted manner; the veterans of the herd directing the movements of the hostile band, and one, by a deeper grunt, not ill-resembling the word of command of a certain general, *de grege porcus*, of our acquaintance, giving dreadful notes of preparation, as if to spirit on the line to a charge.

We made our way with difficulty through the rotten and yielding morass, leaping from tuft to tuft, and risking, by a false slip, to plunge into a bottomless abyss, while our bloodthirsty pursers, with their long legs and lanky sides, and tucked-up bellies, advanced—a fearful phalanx, in semilunar curve, momently gained ground! My friend, who was more accustomed to the bogs than myself, soon outstripped me, not daring to look behind. Once, and only once, did I, and beheld them coming on like a pack of hounds in full cry, and with the scent breast high, and to my horror, perceived the two horns or wings of the troop, making an *echellon* movement in an ever-narrowing circle, like a regiment of cavalry bringing their right and left shoulders forward, to outflank, and then enclose us. I dared not risk a second glance at my foes, but the hoarse voices of the ringleaders ran through the ranks, and I heard and saw the plash of their many feet, as they turned up the mud but a few yards in my rear.

How I reached the hut I know not, but reach it I did, where I found my friend leaning against the wall, breathless with terror. The shed was rudely constructed of peat, and appeared to have been long deserted, consisting only of bare walls and a few rafters; but, providentially, there was a door hanging by one hinge; this I contrived to shut just as the centre of the herd arrived at the threshold. They made a halt, retired a few paces, and collected together, as if to hold a council of war. While they were undecided how to act, we discharged our four barrels loaded with small shot, from the window, at the nearest, which slowly limping, with a sullen grunt of disappointment, the whole of their comrades at their heels, retreated into the covert.

"Thank God!" said R—, when he saw the last disappear among the aloes. "It is but a year since a traveller crossing the Maremma, paid for the journey with his life. There was not a tree to shelter him; and though he was a determined man, and well-armed, and no doubt made a gallant resistance, they hemmed him in and devoured him. I could show you the spot where the swineherds drove them from his mangled remains; it was pointed out to me the last time I came here.

A Kentuckian's Fight with a Panther.

I NEVER was down-hearted but once in in my life, and that was on seeing the death of a faithful friend, who lost his life in trying to save mine. The fact is, I was one day making tracks homeward, after a long tramp through one of our forests—my rifle carelessly resting on my shoulder—when my favorite dog, Sport, who was trotting quietly a-head of me, suddenly stopped stock still, gazed into a big oak tree, bristled up his back, and fetched a loud growl. I looked up, and saw upon a quivering limb,

(98)

a half-grown panther, crouching down close, and in the very act of springing upon him. With a motion quicke" than chain-lightning I levelled my rifle, blazed away, and shot him clean through and through the heart. The varmint, with teeth all set and claws spread, pitched sprawling head foremost to the ground, as dead as Julius Cæsar! That was all fair enoueh; but mark, afore I had hardly dropped my rifle, I found myself thrown down on my profile by the old she-panther, who that minute sprung from an opposite tree and lit upon my shoulders, heavier than all creation! I feel the print of her teeth and nails now! My dog grew mighty loving—he jumped a-top and seized her by the neck; so we all rolled and clawed, and a pretty considerable tight scratch we had of it.

I began to think my right arm was about chawed up; when the varmint finding the dog's teeth rayther hurt her feelings, let me go altogether, and clenched him. Seeing at once that the dog was undermost, and that there was no two ways about a chance

of a choke-off, or let up about her, I just
out jack-knife, and with one slash, prehaps
I didn't cut the panther's throat deep
enough for her to breathe the rest of her
life without nostrils. I did feel mighty sa-
vagerous, and, big as she was, I laid hold
of her hide by the back with an alligator-
grip, and slung her against the nearest tree,
hard enough to make every bone in her
body flash fire. "Thar," says I, "you tar-
nal varmint, root and branch, you are what
I call used up!"

But I turned round to look for my dog,
and—and—and tears gushed into my eyes,
as I see the poor affectionate cretur—all of
a gore of blood—half raised on his fore legs,
and trying to drag his mangled body towards me; down he dropped—I run up to
him, whistled loud, and gave him a friendly
shake of the paws, (for I loved my dog.) But
he was too far gone; he had just strength
enough to wag his tail feebly—fixed his
closing eyes upon me wishfully—then gave
a gasp or two, and—all was over!

NATURAL TUNNEL.

The Natural Tunnel.

The Natural Tunnel is in the south-west-ern part of Virginia, three hundred and fifty-six miles from Richmond, near the line of Tennessee. It is about four hundred and fifty feet in length. A stream of water passes through it, and a stage road over it. In some places the roof is estimated to be about nine hundred feet above the stream; and it bears a striking resemblance to a dome. The tunnel has entrances very different in appearance. At the lower entrance, the deep gorge through which the creek passes, is bounded on three sides by a perpendicular wall of rock, over three hundred feet in height; the fourth side being open to allow the passage of the creek after it leaves the tunnel. The rocks at this place have several small caves or

9*   (101)

fissures, in which the nitrous earth, from which salt petre is extracted, have been found. One or more of these are in the sides of the tunnel itself. During the war of 1812, when saltpetre was very scarce, a small fissure in the wall of rock, attracted attention, and it was determined to explore it. An adventurous individual, by the name of George Dotson, was accordingly lowered from the top by a rope running over a log, and held by several men. The rope not being sufficiently long, the last length, which was tied around his waist, was made of the bark of leatherwood. When down to the level of the fissure, he was still twelve or fifteen feet from it horizontally, being thrown so by the overhanging of the wall of rock. With a long pole, to which was attached a hook, he attempted to pull himself to the fissure. He had nearly succeeded, when the hook slipped, and he swung out into the middle of the ravine, pendulum-like, on a rope of perhaps one hundred and fifty feet in length. Returning on his fearful vibration, he but managed to ward himself off with his pole from being dashed against the rock, when away he swung again.

One of his companions, stationed on the opposite side of the ravine to give directions, instinctively drew back, for it appeared to him that he was slung at him across the abyss. At length the vibrations ceased. At that juncture, Dotson heard something crack above his head: he looked, and saw that a strand of his bark rope had parted. Grasping, with both hands, the rope immediately above the spot, he cried out hastily, "Pull, for —— sake pull!"

On reaching the top he fainted. On another occasion, the bark rope being replaced by a hempen one, he went down again and explored the cave. His only reward was the satisfaction of his curiosity. The hole extended only a few feet.

The natural Tunnel is much visited by travellers. The grandeur of the surrounding scenery attracts many who have not the curiosity to explore the tunnel.

Hair-breadth Escape of a Kentuckian.

THE manner in which dogs have exerted themselves to save the lives of their masters is very remarkable. The following occurs in a work called "Random Sketches of a Kentuckian."

(104)

This Kentuckian sportsman had a favorite stag-hound, strong and of first-rate qualities, named Bravo, which he on one occasion in going on a hunting expedition left at home; taking in his stead on trial a fine-looking hound which had been presented to him a few days before. Having gone a certain length into the woodlands in quest of game, he fired at a powerful stag, which he brought down after a considerable run, and believed to be dead. The animal, however, was only stunned by the shot. On stooping down to bleed him, he was no sooner touched with the keen edge of the knife, than he rose with a sudden bound, "threw me from his body," says the hunter, "and hurled my knife from my hand. I at once saw my danger, but it was too late. With one bound he was upon me, wounding and almost disabling me with his sharp horns and feet.

"I seized him by his wide-spread antlers, and sought to regain possession of my knife, but in vain; each new struggle drew us farther from it. My horse, frightened at the unusual scene, had madly fled to an adjoining ridge, were he stood looking down upon the combat, trembling and quivering in every limb. My dog had not come up, and his bay I could not now hear. The struggles of the furious animal had become dreadful, and every moment I could feel his sharp hoofs cutting deep into my flesh; my grasp upon his antlers were growing less firm, and yet I relinquished not my hold. The struggle had brought us near a deep ditch, washed by autumn rains, and into this I endeavored to force my adversary; but my strength was unequal to the effort: when we approached to the very brink, he leaped over the drain. I relinquished my hold and rolled in, hoping thus to escape him; but he returned to the attack, and throwing himself upon me, inflicted numerous severe cuts upon my face and breast before I could again seize him. Locking my arms round his antlers, I drew his head close to my breast, and was thus, by great effort, enabled to prevent his doing me any serious injury. But I felt that this could not last long; every muscle and fibre of my frame was called into action, and human nature could not long bear up under such exertion. Faltering a silent prayer to Heaven, I prepared to meet my fate.

At this moment of despair I heard the faint bayings of the hound; the stag too heard the sound, and, springing from the ditch, drew me with him. His efforts were now redoubled, and I could scarcely cling to him. Yet that blessed sound came nearer. O how wildly beat my heart as I saw the hound emerge from the ravine, and spring forward with a short, quick bark, as his eye rested on his game. I released my hold of the stag, who turned upon the new enemy. Exhausted, and unable to rise, I still cheered the dog that, dastard like, fled before the infuriated animal, which, seemingly despising such an enemy, again threw himself upon me. Again did I succeed in throwing my arms around his antlers, but but not until he had inflicted several dangerous wounds upon my head and face, cutting to the very bone.

"Blinded by the flowing blood, exhausted and despairing, I cursed the coward dog, which stood near, baying furiously, yet refusing to seize his game. O how I prayed for Bravo! The thoughts of death were bitter. To die thus in the wild forest, alone, with none to help! Thoughts of home and friends coursed like lightning through my brain. At that moment, when hope herself had fled, deep and clear over the neighboring hill came the baying of my gallant Bravo! I should have known his voice among a thousand. I pealed forth, in one faint shout, "On, Bravo, on!" The next moment, with tiger-like bounds, the noble dog come leaping down the declivity, scattering the dried autumnal leaves like a whirlwind in his path. No pause he knew; but, fixing his fangs in the stag's throat, he at once commenced the struggle.

"I fell back, completely exhausted. Blinded with blood, I only knew that a terrific struggle was going on. In a few moments all was still, and I felt the warm breath of my faithful dog as he licked my

wounds. Clearing my eyes from gore, I
saw my late adversary dead at my feet, and
Bravo, 'my own Bravo,' as the heroine of a
modern novel would say, standing over me.
He yet bore around his neck a fragment of
the rope with which I had tied him.   He
had gnawed it in two, and following his
master through all his windings, arrived
in time to rescue him from a most horrible
death."

The Fox Hunters.

Among the gentry of England, fox hunting has long been a favorite amusement. Most of those who have country seats, keep packs of dogs, and horses of noble breed; and occasionally in the proper season, get up large hunting parties. The sport requires fine horsemanship, and a complete knowledge of the habits and inclination of the fox. Nothing can be more invigorating

(110)

THE SQUIRE AND OLD BARNES'S FAMILY.

than the fleet chase, through the woods
and over the fields, with the hounds in full
cry, and the scampering game often ir
sight. The blood bounds through the veins,
and every nerve is strained in the exercise.

Mr. Robert Higginson, or rather Squire
Higginson, as he was generally called, was
one of the wealthiest landlords of the county
of Kent, in England.   He was in the prime
of life, with plenty of leisure, and plenty of
every thing at command.   He always had
his mansion filled with company, feasting,
dancing, and arranging and prosecuting all
sorts of schemes for recreation.   Fox hunting was the Squire's favorite sport.   He
preferred it beyond all in-door amusements,
and was ever delighted when the season
for fox hunting came round.   No one had
a better breed of dogs, or fleeter horses,
and no one took more pride in displaying
them.

One morning, in October, a numerous
party was assembled at the Squire's mansion, preparatory to starting upon a hunt.
A finer day for the sport could not have

been desired. It was clear, cool, and bracing. The gentlemen were soon upon horseback, and the game-keeper was sent forward to start the fox. Presently, the dogs caught sight of the animal as it flew across a field not far from the mansion, and set off, with their usual chorus. Away went the hunters upon their noble steeds, skimming across the meadows, leaping fences and ditches, and running a hundred risks, without the slightest dread. Miles were traversed within a very short time. At length the fox was earthed, and the most violent part of the pursuit was over. But an accident somewhat marred the delight of the hunters. By a sudden plunge of his horse, the Squire was thrown off against a tree, and not only stunned but severely bruised. The fox was forgotten in the anxiety for the Squire, but some of the attendants managed to secure it, after ascertaining that their master was not dangerously injured. Happily, old John Barnes's house was near the place where the accident occurred. Barnes was one of the oldest of the Squire's tenants, and bore the reputation of keeping an open door, a good table, and the best ale. Thither the Squire was led, while the rest of the party returned to the mansion, at his request.

A cheerful scene was soon presented in the cottage of old John Barnes. A blazing fire was upon the hearth, near which sat the hale old man and his wife, while their children and grandchildren were crowding into the small room, to get a sight of the Squire, and to hear what he had to say. Higginson felt rather sore about the head and shoulder, but as he looked upon the scene before him, a smile lit up his face, indicating that the view of such comfort and happiness touched his warm heart. He refused to eat any thing, in spite of the pressing invitation of Barnes and his wife, and the children in chorus. But the ale he took with thanks. He would have all the grown ones drink a toast with him. When the glasses were filled, he proposed, "Health and comfort—a cheerful blaze and a well-filled board—to honest industry." This was drunk with enthusiasm by the grateful cotters. The Squire then chatted awhile, about the condition of things in the cottage, but suddenly seemed to fall into serious reflection. No one ventured to ask for the cause, though nearly all marked the change in his manner.

Some friends of the Squire now arrived, and he accompanied them to his mansion. From that time forward, there was a great change at Higginson's house. Parties were less frequent; and the Squire remained more at home. Very soon a wife was added to the attractions of that home. The tenants were treated with care and generosity, and the Squire seemed to find his chief pleasure in rendering every fireside cheerful.

What had worked this change? The visit to the cottage of old John Barnes. The sight of so much quiet comfort had induced him to seek to find an imitation of it in his own mansion. He ever regarded the accident upon the fox-hunt as a real blessing— as a key that opened to him purer joys than any he had before known. Riot and revelry were excluded from Higginson's house, during his life, and thus a fine estate was saved from ruin; and the time which had been thus spent was given to the improvement of his fellow creatures.

The Hunter's Friendship.

JOSHUA FLEEHART was one of the earliest white hunters upon the north side of the Ohio river. A more fearless and skilful woodsman never roamed the wilderness. He wished for no other companion than his dog; and with him he would traverse districts swarming with enemies, as recklessly as if he was in the midst of friends. Fleehart was a man of large frame, with sinews

(113)

DEERFOOT A PRISONER.

like steel. He was almost as swift of foot as the deer. His rifle was too heavy for the use of common hunters. He was well-known to the Indians of various tribes, and they dreaded and respected his courage and woodcraft.

Flechart never had the highest opinion of the red men. He considered himself equal to a whole tribe of them. But there was one young Shawanee, named Deerfoot, who by a timely service, when the life of Fleehart was in danger, had won the hunter's heart. Whenever he would bring himself to seek a companion for long hunting excursions, he invited Deerfoot, who never refused to take advantage of the opportunity thus offered to learn the mysteries of hunting, and renew the ties of friendship. Fleehart never liked the Shawanee tribe; the Delawares were his constant friends. He often visited their village, and partook of their hospitality. His attachment to Deerfoot thus became the more remarkable.

In the height of this singular friendship, war was kindled between the Delawares and the Shawanees. Deerfoot, of course, had to fight upon the side of his tribe. After a short struggle with his feelings of hatred of the Shawanees, and love for Deerfoot, Flechart determined to remain neutral, and so took occasion to inform both tribes, in order to secure himself from surprise. The war was carried on with various success. Many brave warriors won fame by displaying their prowess, and many sank upon the earth to rise no more. Deerfoot astonished both tribes by his activity and success. He became a terrible foe to the Delawares, and they were very anxious to take or destroy him. At length their vindictive feelings were gratified. In a daring attack upon a Delaware village, Deerfoot was repulsed; and he fell into the hands of his foes. His doom was certain. He was to be tortured to death at the stake. But he determined to die like an Indian hero, defying the torments of the hated Delawares. He was brought to the stake, and old and young, male and female, crowded round, and tried to provoke a complaint from him. But the lips of Deerfoot was curled in scorn, and his eye glanced nothing but resolute defiance. He was painted and tied to the post, there to remain till the next day, when the work of death was to begin.

But a friend was nigh—a priceless friend in time of need. Fleehart heard of the capture of Deerfoot, and determined, even at the risk of sacrificing the terms on which he lived with the Delawares, to save his life. Having formed this resolution, it was necessary for the hunter to devise a plan and put it into instant execution. Persuasion he knew would fail to touch the hearts of the Delawares. Their captive was too important for them to listen to arguments for his release. A bold movement was necessary.

The hunter was intimately acquainted with the Indian custom, and he calculated that he could reach the village before daybreak, upon the morning intended for the torture. He hurried from his hunting ground; and by a march astonishingly rapid, arrived at the village about three hours before day might be expected to dawn. The Delawares were wrapped in slumber.

A few of the stoutest, who had been commissioned to guard the captive, lay upon the ground not far from the fatal stake. Feeling secure from attack, they had fallen into a dose. Deerfoot appeared to be sunk in meditation upon his approaching death. He had lost all hope. Occasionally, he would look up at the star-sown sky, as if to bid it farewell, or to seek in its depths, a confirmation of his creed of a future life in the "happy hunting grounds." Suddenly a man sprang up beside him, cut the thongs that bound him — almost as quick as thought, bade him fly for his life, and thrust a tomahawk into his hands. The man was Fleehart. Deerfoot recognised him, gave him an embrace, took the offered weapon, and sprang towards the woods, followed by the bold hunter. The sound of flying feet aroused the guards. They jumped up just in time to see the skirt of Fleehart's hunting shirt, as he plunged into the wood. A yell rang through the air, and the village started

into life. Twenty warriors were soon in
pursuit. But Flechart and his friend were
not only too far in advance, but they knew
the country, and how to mislead an enemy
in it much better than their pursuers. The
friends were soon beyond the reach of
danger.

The Delawares returned to their village,
vowing to make Flechart feel how dangerous it was thus to tear an enemy from their
power. The hunter was careful to keep out
of their way, until the war was over, when
an explanation of his motives for saving
Deerfoot secured him the attachment of the
Indians, whose nature it was to admire a
firm and devoted friendship.

Sir Robert Gillespie and the Tiger.

Courage is a quality of great importance in a horse, and some possess it in a high degree. It is worthy, too, of remark, that there is often something more than mere natural indifference to danger, something of an intellectual character in the courage of the horse. He *learns* to overcome his fears. At the sight of a tiger, a horse has been known to become wholly paralysed with terror, and incapable of resistance, or even of flight; and yet this instinctive dread of mortal foes can be eradicated by education, and a reliance on the protection of man.

A remarkable proof of this is, that the hunting leopard is allowed by the well-trained horse to spring on his back, either behind or before his master, when he goes

SIR ROBERT GILLESPIE SPEARING THE TIGER.

a-field in pursuit of game. One of the most signal instances of courage on the part of horse and rider, and of perfect concert between both, is that recorded of the late Sir Robert Gillespie and his Arab. Sir Robert being present on the race-course of Calcutta during one of the great Hindoo festivals, when many thousands are assembled to witness all sorts of shows, was suddenly alarmed by the shrieks and commotion of the crowd.

On being informed that a tiger had escaped from his keepers, he immediately called for his horse, and, with no other weapon than a boar-spear snatched from one of the by-standers, he rode to attack this formidable enemy. The tiger was probably amazed at finding himself in the middle of such a number of shrieking beings flying from him in all directions; but the moment he perceived Sir Robert, he crouched in the attitude of preparing to spring upon him; and that instant the gallant soldier passed his horse in a leap over the tiger's back, and struck the spear through his

I

spine. It was a feat requiring the utmost conceivable unity of purpose and movement on the part of horse and rider, almost realising for the moment the fable of the centaur. Had either swerved or wavered for a second, both had been lost. But the brave steed knew his rider. The animal was a small grey, and was afterwards sent home as a present to the Prince Regent.

Sir Robert fell subsequently at the storming of Kalunga. Another horse of his, a favorite black charger, bred at the Cape of Good Hope, and carried by him to India, was at the sale of his effects, competed for by several officers of his division, and finally knocked down to the privates of the 8th dragoons, who contributed their prize money, to the amount of £500 sterling, to retain this commemoration of their beloved commander.

The charger was always led at the head of the regiment on a march, and at the station of Cawnpore was usually indulged with taking his ancient post at the color stand, where the salute of passing squadrons was given at drill and on reviews. When the regiment was ordered home, the funds of the privates running low, he was bought for the same sum by a gentleman, who provided funds and a paddock for him, where he might end his days in comfort; but when the corps had marched, and the sound of the drum had departed, he refused to eat, and on the first opportunity, being led out to exercise, he broke from his groom, and galloping to his ancient station on the parade, after neighing aloud, dropped down and died.

Whaling off New Zealand.

DIEFFENBACH, a German traveller, who visited New Zealand, some years ago, thus speaks of the whaling off those islands:—
The whale-boats are admirably adapted for the purpose for which they are intended. They are of various construction, and are designated as English, French, or American: each has some peculiarity to recommend it. They are capable of resisting the rough sea of Cook's Straits, but are at the same time

(132)

swift and buoyant. When starting on a whaling expedition, the boats leave Te-awa-iti before the dawn of the morning. Each has five or six oars, and a crew accordingly. The boat-stearer and the headsman are the principal men in the boat, and are generally Europeans; the rest are natives. They pull to the entrance of Tory Channel, where a view opens over Cook's Straits and Cloudy Bay from the southern headland, where they keep a "look-out" for the spouting of a whale. The boat which kills the calf claims the cow, even though it should have been killed by another boat's crew.

If a whale has been killed, the different boats assist each other in towing it to Te-awa-iti. I once saw ten or twelve boats towing in a whale. Each boat had a little flag, and the whole scene was gay and animated. One day a calf had been killed, and the cow, having been fastened upon, but not despatched, was towed inside the channel. Gasping in the agonies of death, the tortured animal, when close to our ship, threw up jets of blood, which dyed the sea all around; and, beating about with its tail, it broke a boat right in the middle, and threw the crew into the water; but it at length died, exhausted from the many wounds which the irons and harpoons had inflicted. The calf was stated by the whalers to be six weeks old, and was twenty-four feet long. It was cut up in a few minutes, and gave several barrels of oil. The process was so rapid, that when I came ashore I found only the head. I cut out the brains, the weight of which, amounting to five pounds and one ounce, astonished me greatly. The whalebone was very soft, and therefore useless. There were two hundred plates of it on each side of the roof of the upper jaw. I got the whole roof cut off, and, intending to dry and preserve, I placed it on the roof of a native house; but on the following morning I had the mortification to find that the rats and native dogs had found their way to it in the night, and had eaten all the soft parts, so that the rest fell to pieces. A portion of the heart of this calf was roasted and sent to our table. In taste I

found it very like beef, but it was darker
in color.　The cow was sixty feet long, and
measured between the fins on the belly
eighty-two inches.　Her skin was a velvet-
like black, with the exception of a milk-
white spot round the navel.

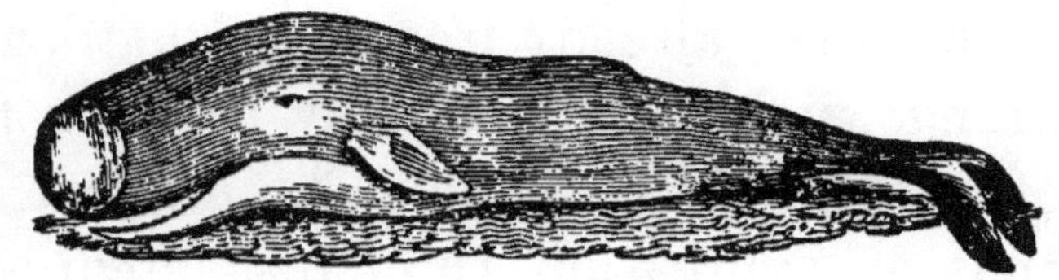

The Arein, or Avalanche.

THE following account of a well-known
and much dreaded phenomenon in Switzer-
land, is given by Mrs. Strutt. The Jaman
is sometimes in the winter and spring a
dangerous passage, as well on account of
the depth of the snow, as in being subject
to avalanches, and to the peculiar *tourmente*,
as the mountaineers expressively term the
snowy winds or windy snows, called the
arein, a word which signifies in the patois
of the country a sandy snow, the particles
thereof being dry and brittle. These *areins*
are formed by one layer of snow falling
upon another, already frozen and hard, and
a strong wind forcing its way between the
two, slicing off, if 1 may be allowed so
homely an expression, the latest fallen and
uppermost, and driving it down the inclined
and icy plain on which it has sought its
short repose, with a fury that sweeps before

it trees, chalets, herds, human beings, all in one bewildering, blinding hurricane, condemning the unfortunate passenger to death.

In 1767, one of these arcins swept away, between the Jamen and the village of Allieres, in Fribourg, on which we were now looking down in all the serenity of a summer's day, a number of large firs and several houses, which it carried to the verge of the precipices washed by the Hongrin in the Gruyeres, sawing the cabaret of Allieres literally in two, and carrying away the upper story, to the amazement of the inmates, who were thus ejected from the attics to the ground-floor without a moment's notice to quit. When any accident fatal to life occurs on the Jamen, it is forbidden to remove the body until the arrival of a magistrate, excepting the mother be present, in which case her sanction is deemed sufficient. The presence of the father is not considered equal authority. There is something very touching in this deference to maternal feeling.

A Prairie Trading Caravan.

Council Grove derives its name from the practice among the traders, from the commencement of the overland commerce between the United States and Mexico, of assembling there for the appointment of officers, and the establishment of rules and regulations to govern their march through the country to the south of it. Mr. Farnham, a diligent traveller in the western country, gives the following description of the proceedings at this place:—The party first elect their commander-in-chief. His duty is to appoint subordinate leaders, and to divide the owners and men into watches, and to assign them their several hours of duty in guarding the camp during the remainder of the perilous journey. He also divides the caravan into two parts, each of which forms a column when on the march.

(133)

MEXICAN SOLDIERS PREPARING TO ATTACK A CARAVAN.

In these lines he assigns each team the place in which it must always be found. Having arranged these several matters, the council breaks up; and the commander, with the guard on duty, moves off in advance to select the track and anticipate approaching danger. After this guard the head teams of each column lead off about thirty feet apart, and the others follow in regular lines, rising and dipping gloriously; two hundred men, one hundred wagons, eight hundred mules; shoutings and whippings, and whistlings and cheerings, are all there; and, amidst them all, the hardy Yankee moves rapidly onward to the siege of the mines of Montezuma. Several objects are gained by this arrangement of the wagons. If they are attacked by the Cumanche cavalry or other foes, the leading teams file to the right and left, and close the front; and the hindmost by a similar movement, close the rear; and thus they form an oblong rampart of wagons laden with cotton goods, that effectually shield teams and men from the small arms of the

Indians. The same arrangement is made when they halt for the night. Within the area thus formed are put, after they are fed, many of the more valuable horses and oxen. The remainder of the animals are "staked," that is, tied to stakes, at a distance of twenty or thirty yards around the line. The ropes by which they are fastened are from thirty to forty feet in length, and the stakes to which they are attached are carefully driven, at such distances apart as shall prevent their being entangled one with another. Among these animals the guard on duty is stationed, standing motionless near them, or crouching so as to discover every moving spot upon the horizon of night.

The reasons assigned for this are, that a guard in motion would be discovered and fired upon by the cautious savage before his presence could be known; and further, that it is impossible to discern the approach of an Indian creeping among the grass in the dark, unless the eye of the observer be so close to the ground as to bring the whole surface lying within the range of vision between it and the line of light around the lower edge of the horizon.   If the camp be attacked, the guard fire and retreat to the wagons.   The whole body take positions for defence ; at one time sallying out, rescue their animals from the grasp of the Indians, and at another, concealed behind their wagons, load and fire upon the intruders with all possible skill and rapidity.   Many were the bloody battles fought on the trail, and such were some of the anxieties and dangers that attended and still attend the "Santa Fe trade."   Many are the graves, along the track, of those who have fallen before the terrible cavalry of the Cumanches.

Ruins and Rapid Vegetation.

Yucatan is the most interesting portion of Central America. The ruins of cities, which once must have been splendid and populous, are found in many parts of this territory, and afford subjects for investigation to the contemplative and the curious. Mr. Stevens gives the following account of a visit to the remains of the past.

On the 15th, at eleven o'clock, we arrived at the hacienda of Uxmal. It stood in its suit of sombre grey, with cattle-yard, large trees, and tanks, the same as when we left it; but there were no friends of old to welcome us; the Delmonico major-domo had gone to Tobasco, and the other had been obliged to leave on account of illness. The mayoral remembered us, but we did not know him; and we determined to pass

(144)

RUINS OF UXMAL, BY MOONLIGHT.

on and take up our abode immediately in the ruins. Stopping a few minutes to give directions about the luggage, we mounted again, and in ten minutes, emerging from the wood, came out again from the open field, in which, grand and lofty as when we saw it before, stood the House of the Dwarf, but the first glance showed us that a year had made great changes. The sides of the lofty structure, then bare and naked, were now covered with high grass, bushes, and weeds, and on the top were bushes and weeds twenty feet high. The House of the Nuns was almost smothered, and the whole field was covered with a rank growth of grass and weeds, over which we could barely look as we rode through. The foundations, terraces, and tops of the buildings were overgrown; weeds and vines were rioting and creeping on the facades; and mounds, terraces, and ruins were a mass of destroying verdure. A strong and vigorous nature was struggling for mastery over art; wrapping the city in its suffocating embraces, and burying it from sight. It seemed as if the grave was closing over a friend, and we had arrived barely in time to take our farewell. Amid this mass of desolation, grand and stately as it was when we left it, stood the Casa del Gobernador, but with all its terraces covered, and separated from us by a mass of impenetrable verdure. On the left of the field was an overgrown milpa, along the edge of which a path led in front of this building. Following this path, we turned the corner of the terrace, and on the farthest side dismounted, and tied our horses. The grass and weeds were above our heads, and we could see nothing. The mayoral broke a way through them, and we reached the foot of the terrace. Working our way over the stones with much toil, we reached the top of the highest terrace. Here, too, the grass and weeds were of the same rank growth. We moved directly to the wall at the east end, and entered the first open door. Here the mayoral wished us to take up our abode; but we knew the localities better than he did, and, creeping along the front as close to the wall as possible, cutting some of the bushes and tearing apart and trampling down others, we reached the central apartment. Here we stopped. Swarms of bats, roused by our approach, fluttered and flew through the long chamber, and passed out of the doors.

These ruins belong to an unknown period of antiquity. They were probably erected by a race of men greatly superior in civilization and art to the Indians who were found in Central America, at the time of Spanish invasion.

The Tyrolians.

The Tyrol is one of the most picturesque regions in Europe. The valleys are fertile, beautiful, and healthy; the mountains, bold, lofty, and grand. The country is inhabited by a rough, hardy, and industrious peasantry. The religion of the Tyrolians is Catholic, and the people are remarkably devout, and are accustomed to keep all the feasts of the church as holidays. Rifle-shooting and dancing form their principal amusements. "No fete-day," says Murray's 'Hand-Book,' "holiday, or marriage passes off without a rustic ball; such entertainments afford the traveller insight into the manners and customs of the people, and an opportunity of observing the varieties of costume. Those, however, who have formed their notions of a Tyrolese dance

(150)

TYROLIANS.

from a ballet at the opera, will be much disappointed. They will find the dancers assembled in the close low room of an inn, so thronged that it would appear impossible to move, much less dance among the throng; yet no sooner does the music strike up, than the whole is in a whirl; no jostling and confusion occur, and the time of the waltz is kept with the most unerring precision. Instead of the elegant costume of the theatre, with its short petticoats and flying ribands, they will find the lasses decked out in pointed hats, or round fur or woollen caps, or in handkerchiefs tied under their chins, and waists reaching up nearly to their necks. The men often wear Hessian boots, which they strike together with great clatter by way of beating time, every now and then uttering a shrill cry, and leaping round in the air, exactly in the manner of the Highland fling. The enthusiasm, almost most approaching to frenzy, with which the dance is kept up, in spite of the heat and crowd, from noon till night, is truly surprising. The partners often seize each other by the shoulders, in an attitude not unlike hugging; they do not always follow the same monotonous revolution, but at one time the man steps round his partner; at another, lifting her high in the air, he twirls her round on her heel with a rapidity that makes her appear to spin, and then, quickly re-uniting, they resume their circular evolutions with an agility and perseverance truly marvellous.

The Tyrolian boys, with hand organ and marmot, are seen wandering about most of the great cities of Europe.

OSTRICHES.

Hunting Ostriches and Wild Horses.

HUNTING upon the plains of South America is the most exciting sport. But it requires fine horsemanship and sure skill in the use of the lasso, or noose, which is thrown over the heads of the game. Robertson, an English traveller, gives the following account of his hunting adventures upon the plains of Paraguay.

We had taken three brace of birds, when, an ostrich starting before us, Candioti, Jun., gave the war-whoop . of pursuit to his Gaucho followers, and to me the well-known intimation of " Vamos, Senor Don Juan." Off went, or rather flew, the Gauchos; my steed bounded away in their company, and we were now, instead of tracking an invisible bird through tufted grass, in full cry after the nimble, conspicuous, and athletic ostrich.   With his erect and angry eye, towering above all herbage, our game flew from us, by the combined air of wings and limbs, at the rate of sixteen miles an hour. The chase lasted half that time; when an Indian peon, starting a head of the close phalanx of his mounted competitors, whirled his balos, with admirable grace and dexterity, around his head, and with deadly aim flung them over the half-running, half-flying, but now devoted ostrich.   Irretrievably entangled, down came the giant bird, rolling, fluttering, panting; and being in an instant despatched, the company or the field stripped him of his feathers, struck them in their girdles, and left the plucked and mangled carcass in the plain, a prey to the vultures, which were already hovering around us.   We now came upon an immense herd of wild horses, and Candioti, Jun., said, "Now Senor Don Juan, I must show how we tame a colt."   So saying, the word was given for the pursuit of the herd, and off, once more, like lightning started the Gaucho horsemen, Candioti and myself keeping up with them.   The herd consisted of about two thousand horses, neighing and snorting, with ears erect and flowing tails, their manes outspread to the wind, affrighted the moment they were conscious of pursuit.

The Gauchos set up their usual cry; the dogs were left in the distance, and it was not till we had followed the flock at full speed, and without a check, for five miles, that the two headmost peons launched their balos at the horse which each had respectively singled out of the herd. Down to the ground, with frightful somersets, came two gallant colts. The herd continued its headlong flight, leaving behind their two prostrate companions. Upon these the whole band of Guachos now ran in; lazos were applied to tie their legs; one man held down the head of each horse, and another the hind quarters, while with singular rapidity and dexterity other two Gauchos put the saddles and bridles on their fallen, trembling, and nearly frantic victims. This done, the two men who had brought down the colts bestrode them as they still lay on the ground. In a moment the lazos which bound their legs were loosed, and at the same time a shout from the field so frightened the potros, that up they started on all fours, but to their astonishment, each with a rider on his back, rivetted, as it were, to the saddle, and controlling them by means of a never-before-dreamed-of bit in his mouth. The animals made a simultaneous and most surprising vault: they reared, plunged, and kicked; now they started off at full gallop, and anon stopped short in their career, with their heads between their legs, endeavoring to throw their riders. "Que esperanza," "vain hope, indeed!" Immoveable sat the two Tape Indians; they smiled at the unavailing attempts of the turbulent and outrageous animals to unseat them; and in less than an hour from the time of their mounting, it was very evident who were to be the masters.

The horses did their very worst, the Indians never lost either the security or the grace of their seats; till, after two hours of the most violent efforts to rid themselves of their burden, the horses were so exhausted. that, drenched in sweat, with gored and palpitating sides, and hanging down their heads, they stood for five minutes together, panting and confounded, but they made not a single effort to move. Then came the Gaucho's turn to exercise his more positive authority. Hitherto he had been entirely upon the defensive. His object was simply to keep his seat and tire out the horse. He now wanted to move it in a given direction, wayward, zigzag; often interrupted was his course at first, still the Gaucho made for a given point; and they advanced towards it, till at the end of about three hours the now mastered animals moved in nearly a direct line, and in company with the other horses, to the questo, or small subordinate establishment, on the estate to which we were repairing. When we got there, the two horses, which so shortly before had been free as the wind, they tied to a stake of the corral, the slaves of lordly man, and all hope of emancipation was at an end.

A Kangaroo Hunt, in Australia.

THE following lively description of a kangaroo hunt, in Australia, is given by one who had much experience in that singular sport, and whose "Tales of the Colonies" has been widely read. The hunt is sometimes pursued on foot, and sometimes on horseback. The former is generally preferred.

It was just light when the stock-keeper called me, and I wasn't long dressing. I took one of the large pistols that father

said I might have, and the stock-keeper had
a musket, and we had half a damper and a
paper of salt, and I had my big hack-knife,
and so off we went. I do think Hector
knew he was going to have some kangaroo;
for he seemed so glad, and licked his chops,
and Fly wagged her tail, and the morning
was so beautiful, and what do you think,
father? the bird that mother likes to hear
so much is a magpie! it is indeed; for I
saw it, and it's just like an English magpie,
only it sings so beautifully. We walked
over the plain till we came to the hills; the
dogs kept quiet behind us. The stock-
keeper said I might see they had been well
trained; they kept their heads low and their
tails hanging down behind them, as if they
had no life in them; but you should have
seen them when they got sight of a kangaroo, didn't they pluck up! We went on
till we got about four or five miles from the
tents, and then we did not talk, for the
kangaroos are startled at the least noise;
they are just like hares for that.

Then the stock-keeper stood still. He

said to the dogs, "Go find," and then the dogs cantered about around us, going further and further off, till Hector began to smell about very earnestly. "He has got scent," said the stock-keeper; and so he had, for he galloped off with his nose to the ground straight ahead. Fly saw him, and she galloped after. "I think it's a big one," said the stock-keeper, "the dogs seem so warm at it." I was running after them as fast as I could, when the stock-keeper called me to stop. "Stop," said he, "it's of no use for you to run, you could not keep up with them."

"Why, what are we to do?" said I; "if they kill a kangaroo, how can we find it?" "Wait, a bit," said he; "all in good time. If the dogs kill a kangaroo, we shall find him, I'll warrant." So we waited and waited till I was quite tired; and a good while after Hector came back quite slowly, as if he was tired, with Fly following after. The stock-keeper looked at his mouth. "What's that for?" said I. "To see if he **has killed**," said he; "look here, his mouth is bloody, and that's come by killing **a kan-garoo**, you may be sure of it."

Then the stock-keeper stood up, and said to Hector, "Show;" and then Hector trotted off, not fast, but pretty fast, so that I was obliged to trot too to keep up with him; and he trotted on and on till I was rather tired, I dare say for three miles from where we were at first; and on he went, and we following him, till he brought us to a dead kangaroo, close to a little pond of water.

It was a monstrous big one, with such claws on each side of his hind legs; a claw that would rip up a dog in a moment, or a man too, if he got at him. "Good dog," said the stock-keeper; and Hector wagged his tail, and seemed to like to be praised. Then the stock-keeper gave me his gun to hold, and he cut open the kangaroo, and gave the inside to the dogs. Then he skinned the upper part down to the loins, and cut the kangaroo in half, and hung it up in a tree, noting the place; the other half he left on the ground; that is, when he went away from the place, for he would

...ot let the dogs have more than a taste of the blood, lest it should spoil their hunting. "What's to be done now?" said I. "We'll kill another," said the stock-keeper, "if you are not tired." I said I was not tired a bit; so after we had rested a little while, we went on again, the dogs following us as at first.

We saw plenty of brush-kangaroos, but we would not touch them. After we had got a mile or two, the stock-keeper, who had been examining the ground all the way along, said, "I think there are some big ones hereabouts, by the look of the marks; so he said to the dogs, "Go find," as he had said before. Almost directly we saw such a large fellow—I'm sure he was six feet high—he looked at us and at the dogs for a moment, and then off he went.

My gracious! what hops he did give! he hopped with his two hind-legs, with his fore legs in the air, and his tail straight out behind—and wasn't it a tail! it was as thick as a bed-post; and this great tail went wag, wag, up and down, as he jumped,

and seemed to balance him behind. But
Hector and Fly were after him. This time
the stock-keeper ran too, for the ground was
level and clear of fallen timber, and you
could see a good way before you. I had
begun to feel a little tired, but I didn't feel
tired then. Hop, hop, went the kangaroo,
and the dogs after him, and we after the
dogs; and we scampered on till I was quite
out of breath; and the kangaroo was a good
bit before the dogs, when he turned up a
hill. "Now we shall have him," said the
stock-keeper; "the dogs will beat him up-
hill." I wanted my breath, but I kept up,
and we scrambled up the hill, and I thought
the dogs would get him; but the kangaroo
got to the top of the hill first, and when we
got a sight of him, he was bounding down
the hill making such prodigious leaps at
every jump, over every thing, that you could
not believe it if you didn't see it. The dogs
had no chance with him down-hill. "It's
of no use," said the stock-keeper, "for us to
try to keep up with him; we may as well
stay here. He'll lead the dogs a pretty

KANGAROO HUNT.

chase, will that fellow; he's a Boomer, and one of the biggest rascals I ever saw."

So we sat down at the top of the hill, under a gum tree, and there we sat a long time, I don't know how long, until we saw Hector coming up. The stock-keeper looked at his mouth. "He has killed," said he; "but he has got a little scratch in the tussle, and so has Fly. That big chap was almost too much for two dogs." Then he said, "Go show!" and Hector and Fly trotted along straight to where the kangaroo lay, without turning to the right or left, but going over every thing, just as if they knew the road quite well.

We came to a hollow, and there we saw the kangaroo lying dead. Just as the stock-keeper was going to cut him open, I saw another kangaroo not a hundred yards off. "There's another," said I, and the dogs, although they had had a hard battle with the kangaroo lying dead, started off directly. Close to us was a large pond of water, like a little lake. The kangaroo was between the dogs and the lake. Not knowing how to get past, I suppose, he hopped right into the lake, and the dogs went after him. He hopped further into the lake, where the water got deeper, and then the dogs were obliged to swim; but they were game and would not leave their work. When the kangaroo found himself getting pretty deep in the water, he stopped and turned on the dogs; but he could not use his terrible hind-claws: so when one of the dogs made a rise at his throat, (they always try to get hold of the throat,) he took hold of him with his fore-legs, and ducked him under the water.

Then the other dog made a spring at him, and the kangaroo ducked him in the same way. "Well," said the stock-keeper, "I never saw the like of that before; this is a new game." And all the while the dogs kept springing at the kangaroo's throat, and the kangaroo kept ducking them under the water. But it was plain that the dogs were getting exhausted, for they were obliged to swim and be ducked too; while the kangaroo stood with his head and fore-legs out of the water.

"This will never do," said the stock-keeper; "he'll drown the dogs at this rate." So he took his gun from me and put a ball in it. "Now," said he, "for a good shot; I must take care not to hit the dogs." He put his gun over the branch of a dead tree, and watching his time, he fired and hit the kangaroo in the neck, and down it came in the water.

He then called off the dogs, and they swam back to us. "He is such a prime one," said he, "it would be a pity to lose his skin;" so he waded in after him, and dragged him out. "It's a pity," said he, "to lose so much meat, but his hind-quarters would be a bigger load than I should like to carry home; but I must have his skin, and I tell you what, young fellow, you shall have his tail, though I'm thinking it's rather more than you can carry home."

This roused me a bit, to think I couldn't carry a kangaroo's tail; so I determined to take it home, if I dropped, though I must say it was so heavy that I was obliged to rest now and then, and the stock-keeper

carried it a good part of the way for me.
" What shall we do with the meat?" said I.
"What shall we do with it?" said he; "are
you hungry?" "I believe you," said I.
"Then we'll make a dinner off him," said
the stock-keeper.

With that we got together some dry sticks,
and made a fire, and the stock-keeper took
the ram-rod of his musket, and first he cut
a slice of the lean off the loins, which he
said was the tenderest part, and put the
ramrod through it, and then he cut out a
bit of fat, and slid it on after the lean, and
so on a bit of fat and a bit of lean, till he
had put on lots of slices, and so he roasted
them over the fire.

He gave me the ramrod to hold, and
cutting a long slice of bark out of a gum-
tree, made two plates, capital plates, he
said, for a bush dinner. I told you we had
got some salt and some damper, and I was
pretty hungry, as you may suppose, and I
thought it the most delicious dinner I ever
ate. When I had done, I lay down on the
grass, and Hector and Fly came and laid

themselves down beside me, and somehow, I don't know how it was, I fell asleep, I was so tired. I slept a good while, for the stock-keeper said it would have been a sin to wake me, I was in such a sweet sleep. I woke up, however, after a good nap, and felt as if I could eat a bit more kangaroo. But it was getting late, and so we made the best of our way home. We passed by the place where we had killed the kangaroo; so the stock-keeper brought home the hind-quarters and the three skins, and I brought home a tail; and I really don't know which is best, kangaroo steaks or kangaroo steamer.*

* Kangaroo steamer is a stew, made of kangaroo meat and bacon.

Adventures in Abyssinia.

About 1510, Helena, the Queen of Abyssinia, anxious to obtain the alliance of Portugal against the Turks, sent Matthew, an Armenian merchant, ambassador to Lisbon. He went by the circuitous route of India, where his dignity not being at first recognised, he was somewhat roughly treated, and detained several years. When at last, in 1513, he reached Lisbon. After the most favorable reception, he was sent back with a fleet, which, in 1515, proceeded to India under Lope Soarez. The governor, soon after his arrival in India sailed for the Red Sea. The ships, meanwhile, met with so many disasters, that they never reached the port of Masuah.

Soarez quitted the gulf, and the enterprise was not resumed till he was succeeded by a more able commander, named Lope

ABYSSINIAN CHIEF.

M

Sequeira. This officer sailed from Goa on the 13th of February, 1520, and arrived at Masuah on the 24th of April. At the neighboring port of Arkeeko he had an interview with the Baharnagash, who, as vassal to the monarch of Abyssinia, held sway over a wide extent of maritime territory. He gave the Portuguese a cordial welcome, and undertook to convey to court both Matthew and an European embassy. At the head of this mission Sequeira placed Rodrigo de Lima.

The embassy left Arkeeko on the 30th of April, and on the 4th of May arrived at the monastery of St. Michael, which was dependent on a more extensive establishment called Bisan, or that of the Vision. Here they were attacked by an epidemic malady, which proved fatal to the merchant and to one of his countrymen. To escape its malignant influence they hastened forward, first to Bisan and then to Dobarwa, the residence of the Baharnagash, to which he had now returned. On this occasion he received them rather coldly, and not without reluctance afforded them the means of proceeding. The passage, too, of the high and rugged mountains of Tigre was found rather formidable. Violent storms of rain and wind often compelled them to seek shelter under the rocks; while the fury of the torrents and the roaring of the gale through the immense woods could not be heard without alarm. Numerous wild animals stalked around, showing no fear at the presence of man; apes were sometimes seen in bands of several hundreds. On descending into the plain, they found it desolated by the more dreadful scourge of locusts. When the inhabitants saw the air darkened by those destructive insects, they became, it is said, "as dead men," crying out, "We are undone, for the locusts come!" Great numbers of both sexes were observed flying to other districts in search of food, their own lands having been entirely consumed by this dreadful visitation.

Amidst these difficulties and annoyances, the mission slowly reached the southern province of Angote, which they found a delightful region, watered by many streams, and having seedtime and harvest throughout the year. The viceroy invited them to a feast, where they found neither chair, table-cloth, nor towel. Mats were spread on the floor, and a wooden board was covered with round cakes; over which was placed the delicate dish, which Alvarez scarcely dares to mention,—"pieces of raw flesh, with warm blood,"—which the governor and his ladies devoured with delight. But the Portuguese could not allow these dainties to enter their lips. The wine also, or rather hydromel, "walked about with great fury;" the mistress of the house, though concealed behind a curtain, taking an ample share.

While proceeding to the court or camp of the Abyssinian monarch, Alvarez saw the lofty hill on which, by a singular and jealous policy, the princesses of the blood-royal are constantly confined. It was of great extent, begirt by a circuit of lofty and perpendicular cliffs appearing to reach almost to the sky. On its summit was a large plain, whence other hills are interspersed with valleys, of which the most beautiful was chosen as the retreat of the august prisoners. The strangers having approached too near it, were notified of their error by a shower of stones.

After passing through the province of Amhara and Shoa, the embassy, on the 19th of October, came in view of an almost endless range of tents and pavilions overspreading an immense plain. This was the grand array or regal camp of the King of Abyssinia, who, engaged in continual war, had at this time no other capital. They forthwith advanced between two rows of about forty thousand persons, among whom a hundred were constantly employed with whips in their hands to maintain order. On this occasion they saw only the *cabeata*, or chief priest and minister, who conveyed several courteous messages between them and the monarch, whom, however, they neither saw nor heard. But on the 20th they were again sent for, when they observed an elevated seat, which they call a bed, with rich curtains of silk and gold concealing the king from their view, but not preventing their holding some conversation with him. His first address was not altogether cordial; he even showed some jealousy of their motives in coming to Abyssinia; but he listened to their explanations, and at length showed a more friendly disposition. Finally, on the 1st of November, they were admitted to a more formal audience, when a series of large curtains were raised, each richer than the other, till at last the richest of all, was lifted, behind which appeared Prester John seated, in a splendid dress of silk and gold, and holding in his hand a silver cross. This prince, who was David III., is described as a young man of about twenty-three, of low stature, and "of the color of ruddy-apples."

The embassy remained five years in Abyssinia, and then having secured good feeling between the two courts, and induced the emperor to embrace the Catholic religion, it sailed for Europe, with presents and a letter for the King of Portugal. The Portuguese were the first European people to visit the eastern coast of Africa, and their enterprise brought them much wealth.

AN ABYSSINIAN FAMILY.

The Indian and the Bears.

In the neighborhood of the Red river, the grisly bears are very numerous. The chief of a tribe of Indians was returning home from a general council, and had lingered behind his men. When not very far from his hut, he met a bear and two cubs, and knowing the ferocious nature of the animals, was considerably alarmed.

They were so close, however, that he

could not escape; and having no alternative, he attacked them, thinking that if he
should be so fortunate as to shoot the mother, he might succeed in killing the cubs
with the butt-end of his gun. He therefore
took aim, but the gun missed fire, although
he had put in a new flint that morning;
and before he could cock again, the bear
rushed upon him, and struck him such a
blow with one of her paws as to throw him
a distance of several yards. She then ran
up, and seizing his head in her mouth,
stood still. He had the presence of mind
to grasp her throat, and with a sudden
wrench rescued his head from her jaws;
but while he was striving to choke her, one
of the cubs struck down his arm, when fortunately he remembered that he had stuck
a knife into his girdle behind. This he
drew with the quickness of thought; but
while in the act of striking the bear with it,
the same cub caught his hand in its mouth,
and held it fast. He seized the knife, however, with his left hand, and wounded the
old bear in several places, until becoming

exasperated, she struck him down sense
less. When he recovered from his swoon
he found himself alone, with his bowels
partly protruding, and both his temples
lacerated. He bound in his intestines with
his belt, and, after staying the bleeding of
his many wounds, raised himself with difficulty, cocked his gun and began to move
slowly away. But he had not proceeded
ten steps, when the bears, which had been
watching him all the time, sprung upon him.

His gun snapped once more, and he was
entirely at their mercy. The mother again
knocked him down with her paw, and seizing
him, dragged him along, when, from loss of
blood and the concussion of the last blow,
he fainted. On regaining his sensibility,
he bound up his wounds, and believing
himself injured beyond recovery, became
inspired by revenge, and resolved to die in
the attempt to destroy some of his savage.
foes. With great difficulty he got on his
feet, cleaned the flint of his gun, drew his
knife, and looking round, stood resolved to
conquer or perish.

The bears rushed upon him. Unable to take aim, he dropped on one knee, and supported his gun on the other, when the old bear seizing the muzzle in her mouth, he drew the trigger and shot her dead. The cubs, however, remained, and they were scarcely less dangerous, as very little strength now remained in him. However, he succeeded, after inflicting several wounds, in driving them off, and sunk down, despairing of ever rising again. But having lain for some time, he found himself slightly refreshed, and succeeded in crawling to his hut, where he related what had befallen him, and bidding farewell to his family, laid himself down to die.

His friends went in search of the bears, and found the mother dead, and the grass all round clotted with blood. The cubs were traced, and having been severely wounded, were easily destroyed. The mangled Indian having enjoyed a sound sleep for several hours, awoke greatly refreshed, and having been persuaded to allow his wounds to be bound, ultimately recovered.

ELEPHANT HUNTERS.

Hunting Adventures in South Africa.

The interior of South Africa teems with game of all kinds and sizes. Elephants, rhinoceroses, giraffes, lions, hyenas, antelopes of various sorts, buffaloes, and many other animals are there found in their perfection. Adventurous hunters from the Cape colony frequently make long excursions into this region, and though they are forced to encounter many dangers, their toils are better rewarded than in any other part of the world. Some of these bold men have given to the world narratives of their expeditions. Of these the most conspicuous, is Roualeyn Gordon Cumming, whose exploits stamp him as the first of hunters. His first meeting and battle with wild elephants is thus narrated.

I resolved at night to watch the water, and try what could be done with elephants by night-shooting. I accordingly ordered the usual watching hole to be constructed; and having placed my bedding in it, repaired thither shortly after sundown. I had lain about two hours in the hole. when I heard a low rumbling noise like distant thunder, caused, as the Bechuanas affirmed, by the bowels of the elephants which were approaching the fountain. I lay on my back, with my mouth open, attentively listening, and could hear them ploughing up the earth with their tusks.

Presently they walked up to the water,

and commenced drinking within fifty yards of me. They approached with so quiet a step, that I fancied it was the footsteps of jackals which I heard; and I was not aware of their presence until I heard the water, which they had drawn up in their trunks and were pouring into their mouths, dropping into the fountain. I then peeped from my sconce with a beating heart, and beheld two enormous bull elephants, which looked like two great castles, standing before me. I could not see very distinctly, for there was only starlight.

Having lain on my breast some time taking my aim, I let fly at one of the elephants, using the Dutch rifle carrying six to the pound. The ball told loudly on his shoulder, and uttering a loud cry, he stumbled through the fountain, when both made off in different directions. All night large herds of zebras and blue wildebeests capered around me, coming sometimes within a few yards. Several parties of rhinoceroses also made their appearance. I felt a little apprehensive that lions might visit the fountain, and every time that hyenas or jackals lapped the water I looked forth, but no lions appeared. At length I fell into a sound sleep, nor did I again raise my head until the bright star of morn had shot far above the eastern horizon.

On the 27th, as day dawned, I left my shooting-hole, and proceeded to inspect the track of my wounded elephant. After following it for some distance I came to an abrupt hillock, and fancying that from the summit a good view might be obtained of the surrounding country, I left my followers to seek the track, while I ascended. I did not raise my eyes from the ground until I had reached the highest pinnacle of rock. I then looked east, and to my inexpressible gratification I beheld a troop of nine or ten elephants quietly browsing within a quarter of a mile of me. I allowed myself only one glance at them, and then rushed down to warn my followers to be silent.

A council of war was hastily held, the result of which was my ordering Isaac to ride hard to camp, with instructions to return as quickly as possible, accompanied by Kleinboy, and to bring me my dogs, the large Dutch rifle, and a fresh horse. I once more ascended the hillock to feast my eyes upon the enchanting sight before me; and drawing out my spyglass, I narrowly observed the motions of the elephants. The herd consisted entirely of females, several of which were followed by small calves.

Presently, on reconnoitring the surrounding country, I discovered a second herd, consisting of five bull elephants, which were quietly feeding about a mile to the northward. The cows were feeding towards a rocky ridge that stretched away from the base of the hillock on which I stood. Burning with impatience to commence the attack, I resolved to try the stalking-system with these, and to hunt the troop of bulls with dogs and horses. Having thus decided, I directed the guides to watch the elephants from the summit of the hillock, and with a beating heart I approached them. The ground and wind favoring me, I soon gained the rocky ridge towards which they were feeding. They were now within one hundred yards, and I resolved to enjoy the pleasure of watching their movements for a little before I fired. They continued to feed slowly towards me, breaking the branches from the trees with their trunks, and eating the leaves and tender shoots. I soon selected the finest in the herd, and kept my eye on her in particular. At length two of the troop had walked slowly past at about sixty yards, and the one which I had selected was feeding with two others on a thorny tree in front of me.

My hand was now as steady as the rock on which it rested, so taking a deliberate aim, I let fly at her a little behind the eye. She got it hard and sharp just where I aimed, but it did not seem to affect her much. Uttering a loud cry, she wheeled about, when I gave her the second ball, close behind the shoulder. All the elephants uttered a strange rumbling noise, and made off in a line to the northward at a brisk ambling pace, their huge fan-like ears flapping in the ratio of their speed. I did not wait to load, but ran back to the hillock to obtain a view. On gaining its summit, the guides pointed out the elephants; they were standing in a grove of shady trees, but the wounded one was some distance behind with another elephant, doubtless its particular friend, who was endeavoring to assist it.

These elephants had probably never before heard the report of a gun; and, having neither seen nor smelt me, they were unaware of the presence of man, and did not seem inclined to go any farther. Presently my men hove in sight, bringing the dogs; and when these came up I waited some time before commencing the attack, that the dogs and horses might recover their wind. We then rode slowly towards the elephants, and had advanced within two hundred yards of them when, the ground being open, they observed us, and made off in an easterly direction; but the wounded one immediately dropped astern, and the next moment she was surrounded by the dogs, which, barking angrily, seemed to engross her attention.

Having placed myself between her and the retreating troop, I dismounted to fire within forty yards of her, in open ground. My horse, Colesburg, was afraid of the elephants, and gave me much trouble, jerking my arm when I tried to fire. At length I let fly; but, on endeavoring to regain my saddle, Colesberg declined to allow me to mount; and when I tried to lead him, and run for it, he only backed towards the wounded elephant.

At this moment I heard another elephant close behind; and on looking about 1 beheld the "friend," with uplifted trunk, charging down upon me at top speed, shrilly trumpeting and following an old black pointer named Schwart, that was perfectly deaf, and trotted along before the enraged elephant quite unaware of what was behind him. I felt certain that she would have either me or my horse. I however determined not to relinquish my steed, but to hold on to my bridle. My men, who of course

ELEPHANT HUNTING.

kept at a safe distance, stood aghast with their mouths open, and for a few seconds my position was not an enviable one. Fortunately, however, the dogs took off the attention of the elephants; and just as they were upon me I managed to spring into the saddle, where I was safe. As I turned my back to mount, the elephants were so very near that I really expected to feel one of their trunks lay hold of me. I rode up to Kleinboy for my double-barrelled two-grooved rifle; he and Isaac were pale and almost speechless with fright. Returning to the charge, I was soon once more along-side, and, firing from the saddle, I sent another brace of bullets into the wounded elephant. Colesburg was extremely unsteady, and destroyed the correctness of my aim.

The friend now seemed resolved to do some mischief, and charged me furiously, pursuing me to a distance of several hundred yards. I therefore deemed it proper to give her a gentle hint to act less officiously, and accordingly, having loaded, I approached within thirty yards, and gave it her sharp, right and left, behind the shoulder, upon which she at once made off with drooping trunk, evidently with a mortal wound. I never recur to this my first day's elephant shooting without regretting my folly in securing only one elephant. The first was now dying and could not leave the ground, and the second was also mortally wounded, and I had only to follow and finish her; but I foolishly allowed her to escape, while I amused myself with the first, which kept walking backwards, and standing by every tree she passed. Two more shots finished her; on receiving them she tossed her trunk up and down two or three times, and, falling on her broadside against a thorny tree, which yielded like grass before her enormous weight, she uttered a deep hoarse groan and expired. This was a very handsome old cow elephant, and was decidedly the best in the troop. She was in excellent condition, and carried a pair of long and perfect tusks. I was in high spirits at my success, and felt so perfectly satisfied with having killed one, that, although it was still early in the day, and my horses were fresh, I allowed the troop of five bulls to remain unmolested, foolishly trusting to fall in with them next day. How little did I then know of the habits of elephants, or the rules to be adopted in hunting them, or deem it probable that I should never see them more.

Having knee-haltered our horses, we set to work with our knives and assagais to prepare the skull for the hatchet, in order to cut out the tusks, nearly half the length of which, I may mention, is embedded in bone sockets in the fore part of the skull. To cut out the tusks of a cow elephant requires barely one-fifth of the labor requisite to cut out those of a bull; and when the sun went down we had managed by our combined efforts to cut out one of the tusks of my first elephant, with which we triumphantly returned, having left the guides in charge of the carcass, where they volunteered to take up their quarters for the night.

Adventures and Customs of the Calmucks

The Calmucks, a principal branch of the great Mongol stock, are more widely dispersed over the globe than any other, even the Arabs are not excepted. Tribes of this people occur over all the countries of Upper Asia, between 38° and 52° north latitude, and from the most northern bend of the Hoang-ho to the banks of the Volga. They are the "Hippophagi," or eaters of horse-flesh, of Pliny, and the more ancient historians. They have very large settlements in the neighborhood of Taganrok, and there Dr. Clarke had an opportunity of studying their habits and appearance. Calmuck men and women were continually galloping their horses through the streets of the town, or lounging in the public places.

A CALMUCK COURTSHIP.

The women, he says, ride better than the men, and a male Calmuck on horseback looks as if he was intoxicated, and likely to fall off every instant, though he never loses his seat; but the women sit with much ease, and ride with extraordinary skill. We shall see, however, by and by, that the men are better equestrians than the traveller supposed. The ceremony of marriage among the Calmucks is performed on horseback. A girl is first mounted and rides off at full speed. Her lover pursues, and if he overtake her she becomes his wife on the spot, and then returns with him to his tent. But it sometimes happens that the woman does not wish to marry the person by whom she is pursued, in which case she will not suffer him to overtake her; and Dr. Clarke was assured that no instance occurs of a Calmuck girl being thus caught unless she had a partiality for her pursuer. If she dislikes him she rides, in English sporting phrase, "neck or nothing," until she has completely escaped, or until the pursuer's horse is tired out, leaving her at liberty to return, to be afterwards chased by some more favored admirer.

Of all the inhabitants of the Russian empire, the Calmucks are the most distinguished by peculiarity of features and manners. In their personal appearance they are athletic, and very forbidding. Their hair is coarse and black, their language harsh and guttural. The Cossacks alone esteem, and intermarry with them; and these unions sometimes produce women of very great beauty, although nothing is more hideous than a Calmuck. High, prominent, broad cheek bones, widely separated from each other; a flat and broad nose; coarse, greasy, jet black hair; scarcely any eyebrows; and enormous prominent ears, constitute no very inviting portrait. Their persons are indescribably filthy, and their habits loathsome. They eat raw horseflesh, and may be seen tearing it like wild beasts from large bones which they hold in their hands. Sometimes they cook their meat, but not in a manner that would make it much more inviting to an English stomach.

A COSSACK.

They cut the muscular parts into steaks which they place under their saddles, and after they have galloped thirty or forty miles, they find the meat tender and palatable. This is a common practice with them on their journeys. The author of Hudibras alludes to this culinary process in terms more pointed than decorous.

Every body has heard of the fermented liquor called *koumiss*, which the Calmucks, the Tartars, &c., manufacture from the milk of the mare. It is produced by combining with six of warm milk, one part of warm water, and a very little sour milk or old koumiss. The vessel is then covered with a thick cloth and left in a moderately warm place for twenty-four hours, until the whole mass becomes sour. After this it is twice beaten with a stick in the shape of a churn staff, so as perfectly to mix together the thick parts and the thin. This being done the process is complete, and the liquor is ready for drinking.

A subsequent process of distillation obtains from this koumiss an ardent spirit called rack or racky, a name identical with that given to the spirit manufactured in the East Indies. Dr. Clarke found some women in the act of making it. "The still," he says, "was composed of mud or very close clay. For a neck of the retort a cane was used; and the receiver was entirely covered by a coating of wet clay. The brandy had passed over. The woman who had the management of the distillery, wishing to give us a small taste of the spirit, thrust a stick with a small tuft of camel's hair into the receiver, dropped a portion of it on the retort, and waving the instrument above her head, scattered the remaining liquor in the air.

"I asked the meaning of this ceremony, and was told it was a religious custom to give always the first of the brandy which they drew from the receiver to their god. The stick was then plunged into the liquor a second time, when more brandy adhering to the camel's hair, she squeezed it into the palm of her dirty hand, and having tasted the liquor, presented it to our lips."

A recent traveller, Madame de Hell, gives a more pleasing picture of the Calmucks, whom she saw under more favorable circumstances, being the guest of one of their princes. The following is her account of an equestrian entertainment she witnessed:

"The moment we were perceived, five or six mounted men, armed with long lassoos (strong flexible thongs with running nooses) rushed into the middle of the taboon (herd of half wild horses,) keeping their eyes constantly fixed on the young prince, who was to point out the animal they should seize. The signal being given, they instantly galloped forward and noosed a young horse with a long dishevelled mane, whose dilated eyes and smoking nostrils betokened inexpressible terror.

"A light clad Calmuck, who followed them on foot, immediately sprang upon the stallion, cut the thongs that were throttling him, and engaged with him in an incredible contest of daring and agility. It would be impossible, I think, for any spectacle more vividly to affect the mind than that which

now met our eyes. Sometimes the rider
and his horse rolled together on the grass;
sometimes they shot through the air with
the speed of an arrow, and then stopped
abruptly, as if a wall had all at once risen
up before them. On a sudden the furious
animal would crawl on its belly, or rear in
a manner that made us shriek with terror,
then plunging forward again in his mad
gallop, he would dash through the taboon,
and endeavor in every possible way to shake
off his novel burden.

" But this exercise, violent and dangerous
as it appeared to us, seemed but sport to
the Calmuck, whose body followed all the
movements of the animal with so much
suppleness, that one would have fancied that
the same spirit animated both bodies. The
sweat poured in foaming streams from the
stallion's flanks, and he trembled in every
limb. As for the rider, his coolness would
have put to shame the most accomplished
horsemen in Europe. In the most critical
moments he still found himself at liberty
to wave his arms in token of triumph; and

in spite of the indomitable humor of his steed, he had sufficient command over it to keep it almost within the circle of our vision. At a signal from the prince, two horsemen, who kept as close to the daring centaur as possible, seized him with amazing quickness, and galloped away with him, before we had time to comprehend this new manœuvre. The horse, for a moment, stupified, soon made off at full speed, and was lost in the midst of the herd. These performances were repeated several times without a single rider suffering himself to be thrown.

"But what was our amazement when we saw a boy of ten years come forward to undertake the same exploit! They selected for him a young white stallion of great size, whose fiery bounds and desperate efforts to break his bonds, indicated a most violent temper.

"I will not attempt to depict our intense emotions during this new conflict. This child, who, like other riders, had only the horse's mane to cling to, afforded an example of the power of reasoning over instinct and brute force. For some minutes he maintained his difficult position with heroic intrepidity. At last to our great relief, a horseman rode up to him, caught him up in his outstretched arm, and threw him on the croup behind him."

JOE LOGSTON'S FIGHT.

Joe Logston's Fight.

Among the many hunters and rangers who figured in the early history of Kentucky, Joe Logston, or "Big Joe Logston," as he was sometimes called, on account of his great size, was conspicuous for daring and success. As a hunter he had few superiors—and as a warrior, after the Indian fashion, a series of exploits secured him reputation.

The following is an account of one of his most desperate fights. He had stopped for awhile at one of the stations in Kentucky; but becoming tired of such a confined life, he resolved to take to the woods, although he knew the hostile Indians were thick in the neighborhood.

Riding along a path which led to a fort, he came to a fine vine of grapes. He laid his gun across the pommel of his saddle, set his hat on it, and filled it with grapes. He turned into the path, and rode carelessly along, eating his grapes; and the first intimation he had of danger, was the crack of two rifles, one from each side of the road. One of the balls passed through the paps of his breast, which, for a male, were remarkably prominent, almost as much so as those of many nurses. The ball just grazed the skin between the paps, but did not injure the breast-bone. The other ball struck his horse behind the saddle, and he sunk in his tracks. Thus was Joe eased off his horse in a manner more rare than welcome. Still he was on his feet in an instant, with his rifle in his hands, and might have taken to his heels ; and I will venture the opinion that no Indian could have caught him. That, he said, was not his sort. He had never left a battle-ground without leaving his mark, and he had resolved that *that* should not be the first.

The moment the guns were fired, one very athletic Indian sprang towards him with tomahawk in hand. His eye was on him, and his gun to his eye, ready, as soon as he approached near enough to make a sure shot, to let him have it. As soon as the Indian discovered this, he jumped behind two pretty large saplings, some small distance apart, neither of which was large enough to cover his body, and, to save himself as well as he could, he kept springing from one to the other.

Joe, knowing he had two enemies on the ground, kept a look-out for the other by a quick glance of the eye. He presently discovered him behind a tree loading his gun. The tree was not quite large enough to hide him. When in the act of pushing down his bullet, he exposed pretty fairly his hips. Joe, in the twinkling of an eye, wheeled, and let him have his load in the part exposed. The big Indian then with a mighty "Ugh!" rushed towards him with his raised tomahawk. Here were two warriors met, each determined to conquer or die—each the Goliath of his nation. The Indian had rather the advantage in size of frame, but Joe in weight and muscular strength. The Indian made a halt at the distance of fifteen or twenty feet, and threw his tomahawk with all his force, but Joe had his eye on him and dodged it. It flew quite out of the reach of either of them. Joe then clubbed his gun and made at the Indian, thinking to knock him down. The Indian sprang into some brush or saplings, to avoid his blows. The Indian depended entirely on dodging, with the help of the saplings. At length, Joe thinking he had a pretty fair chance, made a side blow with such force, that, missing the dodging Indian, the gun, now reduced to the naked barrel, was drawn quite out of his hands, and flew quite out of his reach. The Indian now gave another exulting "Ugh!" and sprang upon him with all the savage fury he was master of. Neither of them had a weapon in his hands, and the Indian, seeing Logston bleeding freely, thought he could throw him down and despatch him.

In this he was mistaken. They seized each other, and a desperate scuffle ensued. Joe could throw him down, but could not hold him there. The Indian being naked, with his hide oiled, had greatly the advantage in a ground scuffle, and would still slip out of Joe's grasp and rise. After throwing him five or six times, Joe found, that between loss of blood and violent exertions, his wind was leaving him, and that he must change his mode of warfare or lose his scalp, which he was not yet willing to spare. He threw the Indian again, and without attempting to hold him, jumped from him, and as he rose, aimed a fist blow at his head, which caused him to fall back, and as he would rise, Joe gave him several blows in succession, the Indian rising slower each time.

He at last succeeded in giving him a pretty
fair blow in the burr of the ear, with all his
force, and he fell, as Joe thought, pretty
near dead.   Joe jumped on him, and thinking he could despatch him by choking,
grasped his neck with his left hand, keeping his right one free for contingencies. Joe
soon found the Indian was not so dead as
he thought, and that he was making some
use of his right arm, which lay across his
body, and, on casting his eyes down, discovered the Indian was making an effort to
unsheath a knife that was hanging at his
belt.   The knife was short, and so sunk in
the sheath that it was necessary to force it
up by pressing against the point. This the
Indian was trying to effect, and with good
success. Joe kept his eye on it, and let the
Indian work the handle out, when he suddenly grabbed it, jerked it out of the sheath,
and sunk it up to the handle in the Indian's
breast, who gave a death groan and expired.

Joe now thought of the other Indian, and
not knowing how far he had succeeded in
killing or crippling him, sprang to his feet.

He found the crippled Indian had crawled some distance towards them, and had placed his broken back against a log, and was trying to raise his gun to shoot him, but in attempting to do which he would fall forward, and had to push against his gun to raise himself again.

Joe, seeing that he was safe, concluded he had fought long enough for healthy exercise that day, and not liking to be killed by a crippled Indian, he made for the fort. He got in about nightfall, and a hard looking case he was—blood and dirt from the crown of his head to the sole of his foot, no horse, no hat, no gun—with an account of the battle that some of his comrades could scarce believe to be much else than one of his stories in which he would sometimes indulge. He told them to go and judge for themselves. Next morning a company was made up to go to Joe's battle-ground. When they approached it, Joe's accusers became more confirmed, as there was no appearance of dead Indians, and nothing Joe had talked of but the dead horse.   They, however, found a trail, as if something had been dragged away.   On pursuing it they found the big Indian, at a little distance, beside a log, covered up with leaves.   Still pursuing the trail, some hundred yards further, they found the broken-backed Indian, lying on his back, with his own knife sticking up to the hilt in his body, just below the breast bone, evidently to show that he had killed himself, and that he had not come to his end by the hand of an enemy.

They had a long search before they found the knife with which Joe killed the big Indian.   They at last found it forced down into the ground below the surface, apparently by the weight of a person's heel. This had been done by the crippled Indian. The great efforts he must have made, alone, in that condition, show, among thousands of other instances, what Indians are capable of under the greatest extremities.

GRIZZLY BEAR.

Adventure with a Grizzly Bear.

[FROM KELLY'S EXCURSION TO CALIFORNIA.]

I NOW took a long farewell of the horses, and turned northward, selecting a line close in by the base of the hills, going along at an improved pace, with a view of reaching the trading-post the same night; but halting in a gully to look for water, I found a little pool, evidently scratched out by a bear, as there were foot-prints and claw-marks about it; and I was aware instinct prompts that brute where water is nearest the surface, when he scratches until he comes to it. This was one of very large size, the foot-mark behind the toes being full nine inches; and although I had my misgivings about the prudence of a *tete-a-tete* with a great grizzly bear, still the "better part of valor" was overcome, as it often is, by the anticipated honor and glory of a single combat, and conquest of such a ferocious beast. I was well armed, too, with my favorite rifle, a Colt's revolver, that never disappointed me, and a nondescript weapon, a sort of cross between a claymore and a bowie-knife; so, after capping afresh, hanging the bridle on the horn of the saddle, and, staking my mule, I followed the trail up a gully, and much sooner than I expected came within view and good shooting distance of Bruin, who was seated erect, with his side toward me, in front of a manzanita bush, making a repast on his favorite berry.

The sharp click, of the cock causing him to turn quickly round, left little time for deliberation; so, taking a ready good aim at the region of the heart, I let drive, the ball, as I subsequently found, glancing along the ribs, entering the armpit, and shattering smartly some of the shoulder bones. I exulted as I saw him stagger and come to his side; the next glance, however, revealed him, to my dismay, on all fours, in direct pursuit, but going lame; so I bolted for the mule, sadly encumbered with a huge pair of Mexican spurs, the nervous noise of the crushing brush close in my rear convinced me that he was fast gaining on me; I therefore dropped my rifle, putting on fresh steam, and reaching the rope, pulled up the picket-pin, and springing into the saddle with merely a hold of the lariat, plunged the spurs into the mule, which, much to my affright produced a kick and a retrograde movement; but in the exertion having got a glimpse of my pursuer, uttering a snort of terror, he went off at a pace I did not think him capable of, soon widening the distance between us and the bear; but having no means of guiding his motions, he brought me violently in contact with the arm of a tree, which unhorsed and stunned me exceedingly. Scrambling to my feet as well as I could, I saw my relentless enemy close at hand, leaving me the only alternative of ascending a tree; but, in my hurried and nervous efforts, I had scarcely my feet above his reach, when he was right under, evidently enfeebled by the loss of blood, as the exertion made it well out copiously.

After a moment's pause, and a fierce glare upwards from his blood-shot eyes, he clasped the trunk; but I saw his endeavors to climb were crippled by the wounded shoulder. However, by the aid of his jaws, he just succeeded in reaching the first branch with his sound arm, and was working convulsively to bring up the body, when, with a well-directed blow from my cutlass, I completely severed the tendons of the foot, and he instantly fell with a dreadful souse and horrific growl, the blood spouting up as if impelled from a jet; he rose again somewhat tardily, and limping round the tree with upturned eyes, kept tearing off the bark with his tusks. However, watching my opportunity, and leaning downward, I sent a ball from my revolver with such good effect immediately behind the head, that he dropped; and my nerves being rather more composed, I leisurely distributed the remaining five balls in his body.

By this time I saw the muscular system totally relaxed, so I descended with confidence, and found him quite dead, and myself not a little enervated with the excitement and the effects of my wound, which bled profusely from the temple; so much so, that I thought an artery was ruptured. I bound up my head as well as I could, loaded my revolver anew, and returned for my rifle; but as evening was approaching, and my mule gone, I had little time to survey the dimensions of my fallen foe, and no means of packing much of his flesh. I therefore hacked off a few steaks from his thigh, and hewing off one of his hind feet as a sure trophy of victory, I set out toward the trading-post, which I reached about midnight, my friend and my truant mule being there before me, but no horses.

I exhibited the foot of my fallen foe in great triumph, and described the conflict with due emphasis and effect to the company, who arose to listen; after which I made a transfer of the flesh to the traders, on condition that there was not to be any charge for the hotel or the use of the mule. There was an old experienced French trapper belonged to the party, who, judging from the size of the foot, set down the weight of the bear at fifteen hundred pounds, which, he said, they frequently overrun; he himself, as well as Colonel Fremont's exploring party, having killed several that came to two thousand pounds.

He advised me, should I again be pursued by a bear, and have no other means of escape, to ascend a small girthed tree, which they cannot get up, for, not having any central joint in the fore-legs, they cannot climb any with a branchless stem that does not fully fill their embrace; and in the event of not being able to accomplish the ascent before my pursuer overtook me, to place my back against it, when, if it and I did not constitute a bulk capable of filling his hug, I might have time to rip out his entrails before he could kill me, being in a favorable posture for the operation. They do not generally use their mouth in the destruction of their victims, but, hugging them closely, lift one of the hind feet, which are armed with tremendous claws, and tear out the bowels.

The Frenchman's advice reads rationally enough, and is a feasible theory on the art of evading unbearable compression; but, unfortunately, in the haunts of that animal those slim juvenile saplings are rarely met with, and a person closely confronted with such a grizzly *vis-a-vis* is not exactly in a tone of nerve for surgical operations.

A Spanish Bull Fight.

ONE day Don Philippe insisted upon taking us to witness a bull fight, which was about to take place, and which it was reported, the queen herself was expected to attend. This was a spectacle we had never yet beheld, and our curiosity was therefore aroused to the highest possible pitch of excitement. Visions of blood floated before our fancy, and flashing steel glanced across our sight. Anxiety stood on tip-toe, and the moments flew slowly by, until the wished-for hour arrived. We left the business of securing seats in the arena to Philippe, who, by early application, succeeded in obtaining for us as eligible positions for witnessing the spectacle as we could reasonably desire.

(236)

A SPANISH BULL FIGHT.

The critical moment was now at hand, our hearts almost leaped from our mouths, so deeply were we excited in contemplation of the sanguinary event. At length the trumpets sounded, and forthwith entered, in martial array, the entire body of combatants, gayly dressed, and presenting together a most striking and brilliant effect. Marching to the opposite side of the ring, they respectfully bowed to the appointed authorities, and then took their places in complete readiness for action.

At a given signal, a small iron gate was suddenly opened, and in an instant a furious bull bounded frantically into the arena; and then, as if pretrified with astonishment at the wonderful scene around him, he stood motionless for a few seconds, staring wildly at the the immense assembly, and pawing vehemently the ground beneath his feet. It was a solemn and critical moment, and I can truly say I never before experienced such an intense degree of curiosity and interest. My feelings were wound up to the highest pitch of excitement,

and I can scarcely believe that even that
terrible human tragedy, a bloody gladiatorial
scene, could have affected me more deeply.
The compressed fury of the bull lasted but
an instant; suddenly his glaring eye
caught sight of a red flag, which one of the
chulos, or foot combatants, had waved before
him, and immediately he rushed after his
nimble adversary, who evaded his pursuit
by jumping skilfully over the lower enclosure of the ring. The herculean animal,
thus balked in his rage, next plunged des-
perately toward one of the *picadores*, or
mounted horsemen, who calmly and fear-
lessly awaited his approach, and then turned
off his attack by the masterly management
of his long and steel-capped pike. Thwarted
once more in his purpose, he became still
more frantic than before, while his low and
suppressed roar, expressive of the concen-
trated passion and rage which burned within
him, sounded like distant thunder to my
ears. Half closing his eyes, and lowering
his formidable horns, he darted again at
one of the picadores, and with such tremen-

dous power, that he completely unhorsed him. Then shouts of applause from the spectators filled the arena: "Bravo toro!" "Viva toro!" and other exclamations of encouragement for the bull broke from every mouth.

The picador lost no time in springing to his feet and regaining his horse, which, however, could scarcely stand, so weak was the poor creature from the stream of blood issuing from the deep wound in his breast. As soon as the enraged bull, whose attention had been purposely withdrawn by the chulos, beheld his former adversary now crimsoned with gore, he rushed at him with the most terrific fury, and, thrusting his horns savagely into the lower parts of the tottering animal, he almost raised him from his feet, and so lacerated and tore open his abdomen, that his bowels gushed out upon the ground. Unable any longer to sustain himself, the pitiable animal fell down in the awful agonies of death, and in a few moments expired. Two other horses shortly shared the same miserable fate, and their mangled bodies

were lying covered with blood, in the centre
of the arena. The bull himself was now
becoming perceptibly exhausted, and his
own end was drawing nigh.

For the purpose of stimulating and
arousing into momentary action his rapidly
waning strength, the assailants on foot attacked him with barbed darts, called *bande-
rillos*, which they thrust with skill into each
side of his brawny neck. Sometimes these
little javelins are charged with a prepared
powder, which explodes the instant that the
sharp steel sinks into the flesh. The torture thus produced drives the wretched
animal to the extreme of madness, who bel-
lows and bounds in his agony, as if endued
with the energy of a new life.

On the present occasion, the arrows used
were not of an explosive character, yet they
served scarcely less effectually to enrage
the furious monster. But hark! the last
trumpet is sounding the awful death-knell
of the warrior-beast. The ring becomes instantly cleared, and the foaming animal
stands motionless and alone, sole monarch

of the arena.   But the fiat has gone forth,
and the doom of death is impending over
him.   The *matador* enters the ring by a se-
cret door, and, after bowing to the presi-
dent, and throwing down his cap in token
of respect, slowly and deliberately ap-
proaches his terrific adversary, who stands
as if enchained to the spot by a conscious-
ness of the fearful destiny that awaits him.
The matador, undismayed by the ferocious
aspect of the bull, cautiously advances,
with his eyes fixed firmly and magnetically
upon him; a bright Toledo blade glistens
in his right hand, while in his left he car-
ries the *muleta*, or crimson flag, with which
to exasperate the declining spirit of his foe.

An intense stillness reigns throughout
the vast assemblage, the most critical
point of the tragedy is at hand, and every
glance is rivetted upon the person and
movements of the matador.   A single fatal
thrust may launch him into eternity, yet
no expression of fear escapes him; cool,
and self-possessed, he stands before his
victim, studious of every motion, and pre-

pared to take advantage of any chance for the decisive blow.

It is this wonderful display of skill and bravery that fascinates the attention of a Spanish audience, and not the shedding of blood or the sufferings of the animal, which are as much lost sight of in the excitement of the moment as the gasping of a fish or the quivering of a worm upon the hook is disregarded by the humane disciple of Izaak Walton.

The bull and matador, as motionless as if carved in marble, present a fearfully artistic effect. At length, like an electric flash, the polished steel of the matador flies into the air, and descends with tremendous force into the neck of the doomed animal, burying itself in the flesh, even up to the hilt. The blow is well made, and from the mouth of the bull gushes forth a crimson stream: he staggers, drops on his knees, recovers himself for an instant, and then falls dead at the feet of his conqueror, amid the tumultuous plaudits of the excited throng of spectators.

Captain Stedman and the Boa Constrictor

The following adventure occurred during the residence of Captain Stedman in Surinam:—The captain was lying in his hammock, as his vessel floated down the river, when his sentinel told him he had seen and challenged something black, moving in the brushwood on the beach, which gave no answer. Up rose the captain, manned the canoe that accompanied his vessel, and rowed to the shore to ascertain what it was. One of his slaves cried out that it was no negro, but a great snake that the captain might shoot if he pleased. The captain having no such inclination, ordered all hands to return on board. The slave, David, who had first challenged the snake, then begged leave to step forward and shoot it. This seems to have roused the captain, for he

21*   (245)

determined to kill it himself, and loaded with ball cartridge.

The master and slave then proceeded. David cut a path with a bill-hook, and behind him came a marine with three more loaded guns. They had not got above twenty yards through mud and water, the negro looking every way with uncommon vivacity, when he suddenly called out, "Me see snakee!" and, sure enough there the reptile lay, coiled up under the fallen leaves and rubbish of the trees. So well covered was it, that some time elapsed before the captain could perceive its head, not above sixteen feet from him, moving its forked tongue, while its vividly-bright eyes appeared to emit sparks of fire. The captain now rested his piece upon a branch, to secure a surer aim, and fired. The ball missed the head, but went through the body, when the snake struck round with such astonishing force as to cut away all the underwood around it, with the facility of a scythe mowing grass, and, flouncing with its tail, made the mud and dirt fly over their heads to a

A BOA CONSTRICTOR.

considerable distance.   This commotion seems to have sent the party to the right about; for they · took to their heels, and crawled into the canoes. David, however, entreated the captain to renew the charge, assuring him that the snake would be quiet in a few minutes, and that it was neither able nor inclined to pursue them, supporting his opinion by walking before the captain till the latter should be ready to fire.

They now found the snake a little removed from its former station, very quiet, with its head as before, lying out among the fallen leaves, rotten bark, and old moss. Stedman fired at it immediately, but with no better success than at first; and the enraged animal, being but slightly wounded by the second shot, sent up such a cloud of dust and dirt as the captain had never seen, except in a whirlwind; and away they all again retreated to their canoe. Tired of the exploit, Stedman gave orders to row towards the barge; but the persevering David still entreating that *he* might be permitted to kill the reptile, the captain determined to make a third and last attempt in his company; and they this time directed their fire with such effect that the snake was shot by one of them through the head.

The vanquished monster was then secured by a running-noose passed over its head, not without some difficulty, however; for, though it was mortally wounded, it still continued to writhe and twist itself about so as to render a near approach dangerous. The serpent was dragged to the shore, and made fast to the canoe, in order that it might be towed to the vessel, and continued swimming like an eel till the party arrived on board, when it was finally determined that the snake should be again taken on shore, and there skinned for the sake of its oil.

This was accordingly done; and David having climbed a tree with the end of a rope in his hand, let it down over a strong-forked bough, the other negroes hoisted away, and the serpent was suspended from the tree. Then, David quitting the tree, with a sharp knife between his teeth, clung fast upon the suspended snake, still twisting and twining, and commenced ripping the subject up; he then stripped down the skin as he came down.

Captain Stedman acknowledges, that though he perceived that the snake was no longer able to do the operator any harm, he could not, without emotion, see a naked man, black and bloody, clinging with arms and legs round the slimy and yet living monster. The skin and above four gallons of clarified fat, or rather oil, were the spoils secured on this occasion; full as many gallons more seem to have been wasted. The negroes cut the flesh into pieces, intending to feast on it; but the captain would not permit them to eat what he considered disgusting food, though they declared that it was exceedingly good and wholesome. The negroes were right, and the captain was wrong; the flesh of most serpents is very good and nourishing, to say nothing of the restorative qualities attributed to it.

Adventures among the Indians and Gauchos of the Pampas.

WHERE there is such a profusion of horses, the people cannot fail to be all riders; and such they are, bold and expert beyond all comparison with other nations. The Indians of the Pampas and the Prairies, whose fathers fled in horror and dismay from the fatal apparition of the Spanish horses, are now literally "incorporated and demi-natured with the brave beast."

(252)

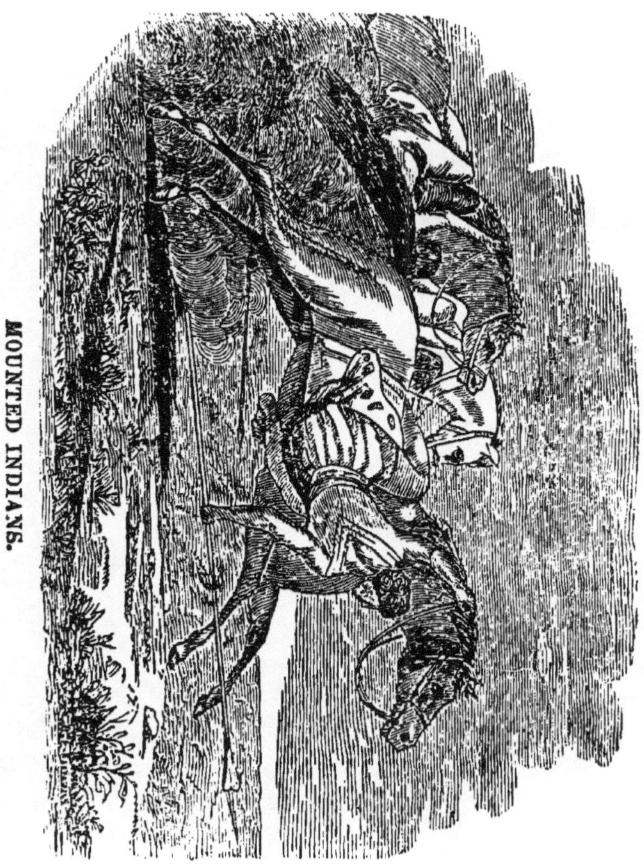

MOUNTED INDIANS.

22

Many of the tribes, from being constantly on horseback from their infancy, can scarcely walk. Their legs have become too weak, from long disuse, for that kind of progression, and they loathe and despise it. The proudest attitude of the human figure, as they declare, is when a man, bending over his horse, lance in hand, is riding at his enemy. The occupation of their lives is war, especially against "the Christians," and they pursue it for two objects,—to steal cattle, and for the pleasure of murdering the people; and they will even leave the cattle to massacre and torture their enemies, such is their ferocity, and their hereditary hatred to the descendants of the cruel oppressors of their fathers.

The Gauchos, who themselves ride so beautifully, declare that it is impossible to vie with a mounted Indian; for that the Indian's horses are better than their own, and also that they have such a way of urging them on by their cries, and by a peculiar motion of their bodies, that even if they were to change horses, the Indians would beat them. Mr. Darwin relates a case in which this fact was proved.

At Cholechel, Bahia-Blanca, General Rosas' troops encountered a tribe of Indians, of whom they killed twenty or thirty. The cacique escaped in a manner which surprised every one; the chief Indians have always one or two picked horses, which they keep ready for any urgent occasion.

On one of these, an old white horse, the cacique sprung, taking with him his little son; the horse had neither saddle nor bridle. To avoid the shots the Indian rode in the peculiar method of his nation, namely, with an arm round the horse's neck, and one leg on its back. Thus hanging on one side he was seen patting the horse's head, and talking with him. The pursuers urged every effort in the chase; the commandant three times changed his horse, but all in vain; the old Indian father and his son escaped, and were free.

What a fine picture one can form in one's mind; the naked bronze-like figure of the old man with his little boy, riding like a

Mazeppa on the white horse, thus leaving far behind him the host of his pursuers!

Colt breaking is managed by the Gauchos, or Guassos, as they are called in Chili, with the lasso, much in the same way as by the Calmucks. Their skill in the use of this instrument is extraordinary, and it was a weapon of great power in their hands during the war of independence. They never failed to dismount cavalry with it, or to throw down the horses of those who came within their reach. There is a well authenticated story of eight or ten Gauchos who had never seen a piece of artillery until one was fired at them in the streets of Buenos Ayres. Notwithstanding the effect of the fire they galloped fiercely up to it, placed their lassos over the cannon, and by their united strength fairly overturned it.

Another anecdote is related of them, which may be true, though it does not rest on such good authority. A number of armed boats were sent to effect a landing at a certain point on the coast guarded solely by these horsemen. The party in the boats caring little for an enemy unprovided with fire-arms, rowed confidently along the shore. The Gauchos meanwhile were watching their opportunity, and the moment the boats came sufficiently near, dashed into the water, and throwing their lassos round the necks of the officers, fairly dragged every one of them out of their boats.

The idea of being thrown, let the horse do what it likes, never enters the head of a Gaucho; a good rider, according to them, is a man who can manage an untamed colt, or who, if his horse falls, alights unhurt on his own feet. "I have heard," says Mr. Darwin, "of a man betting that he would throw his horse down twenty times, and that nineteen out of these he would not fall himself. I recollect seeing a Gaucho riding so very stubborn a horse, which three times reared so excessively high as to fall backwards with great violence. The man judged with uncommon coolness the proper moment for slipping off, not an instant before or after the right time. Directly the horse rose, the man jumped on his back, and at last they started on a gallop. The Gaucho never appears to exert any muscular force. I was one day watching a good rider, as we were galloping along at a rapid pace, and thought to myself, surely if the horse starts, you appear so careless on your seat, you must fall. At this moment a male ostrich sprang from its nest right beneath the nose of the horse. The young colt bounded on one side like a stag; but as for the man, all that could be said was, that he started and took fright as part of his horse.

" In Chili and Peru more pains are taken with the mouth of the horse than in La Plata, and this is evidently in consequence of the more intricate nature of the country. In Chili, a horse is not considered perfectly broken till he can be brought up standing, in the midst of his full speed, on any particular spot; for instance, on a cloak thrown on the ground; or until he will charge a wall, and, rearing, scrape the surface with his hoofs. I have seen an animal bounding with spirit, yet merely reined by a fore-finger and thumb, taken at full gallop across a court-yard, and then made to wheel round the post of a verandah with great speed, but at so equal a distance, that the rider, with outstretched arm all the while, kept one finger rubbing the post; then making a demivolte in the air, with the other arm outstretched in a like manner, he wheeled round in an astonishing force in an opposite direction.

"Such a horse is well broken, and though this at first may appear useless, it is far otherwise; it is only carrying that which is daily necessary into perfection. When a bullock is checked and caught by the lasso, it will sometimes gollop round and round in a circle, and the horse being alarmed at the great strain, if not well broken, will not readily turn like the pivot of a wheel. In consequence many men have been killed; for if the lasso once makes a twist round a man's body, it will instantly, from the power of the two opposed animals, almost cut him in two.

"In Chili, I was told an anecdote which

INDIAN HUNTER.

I believe was true, and it offers a good illustration of the use of a well broken animal. A respectable man, riding one day, met two others, one of whom was mounted on a horse which he knew to have been stolen from himself. He challenged them; they answered by drawing their sabres and giving chase. The man on his good and fleet beast kept just ahead; as he passed a thick bush he wheeled round it, and brought up his horse to a dead check. The pursuers were obliged to shoot on one side and ahead. Then instantly dashing on right behind them, he buried his knife in the back of one, wounded the other, recovered his horse from the dying robber, and rode home.

"For these feats in horsemanship two things are necessary; a most severe bit, like the Mameluke, the power of which, though seldom used, the horse knows full well; and large blunt spurs, that can be applied either as a mere touch, or as an instrument of mere pain. I conceive that with English spurs, the slightest touch of which pricks the skin, it would be impossible to break a horse after the South American fashion."

Nothing is done on foot by the Gauchos that can possibly be done on horseback. Even mounted beggarmen are to be seen in the streets of Buenos Ayres and Mendoza. The butcher, of course, plies his trade on horseback, in the manner thus described by Basil Hall; "The cattle had been driven into an enclosure, or corral, whence they were now let out one by one, and killed; but not in the manner practised in England, where they are dragged into a house, and despatched by blows on the forehead with a poleaxe. Here the whole took place in the open air, and resembled rather the catastrophe of a grand field-sport than a deliberate slaughter. On a level space of ground before the corral were ranged, in a line, four or five Gauchos on horseback, with their lassos in their hands, and opposite them another set of men, similarly equipped, so as to form a wide lane, extending from the gate of the corral to the distance of thirty or forty yards. When all was prepared, the leader of the Gauchos drew out the bars closing the entrance to the corral, and, riding in, separated one from the drove, which he goaded till it escaped at the opening. The reluctance of the cattle to quit the corral was evident, but when at length forced to do so, they dashed forward with the utmost impetuosity. It is said, that in this country, even the wildest animals have an instinctive horror of the lasso; those in a domestic state certainly have, and betray fear whenever they see it. Be this as it may, the moment they pass the gate, they spring forward at full speed with all the appearance of terror. But were they to go ten times faster, it would avail them nothing against the irresistible lasso, which, in the midst of dust and confusion seemingly inextricable, is placed by the Gauchos, with the most perfect correctness, over the parts aimed at.

" There cannot be conceived a more spirited or more picturesque scene than was now presented to us. Let the furious beast be imagined driven almost to madness by

thirst and a variety of irritations, and in
the utmost terror at the multitude of lassos
whirling all around him; he rushes wildly
forward, his eyes flashing fire, his nostrils
almost touching the ground, and his breath
driving off the dust in his course. For one
short instant he is free, and full of life and
strength, defying, as it were, all the world
to restrain him in his headlong course; the
next moment he is covered with lassos; his
horns, his neck, his legs are all encircled
by those inevitable cords, hanging loose, in
long festoons, from the hands of the horsemen, galloping in all directions, but the
next instant as tight as bars of iron, and
the noble animal lying prostrate on the
ground motionless and helpless. He is immediately despatched by a man on foot,
who stands ready for this purpose with a
long sharp knife in his hand; and as soon
as the body is disentangled from the lassos,
it is drawn on one side, and another beast
is driven out of the corral, and caught in
the same manner.

While the more serious business was

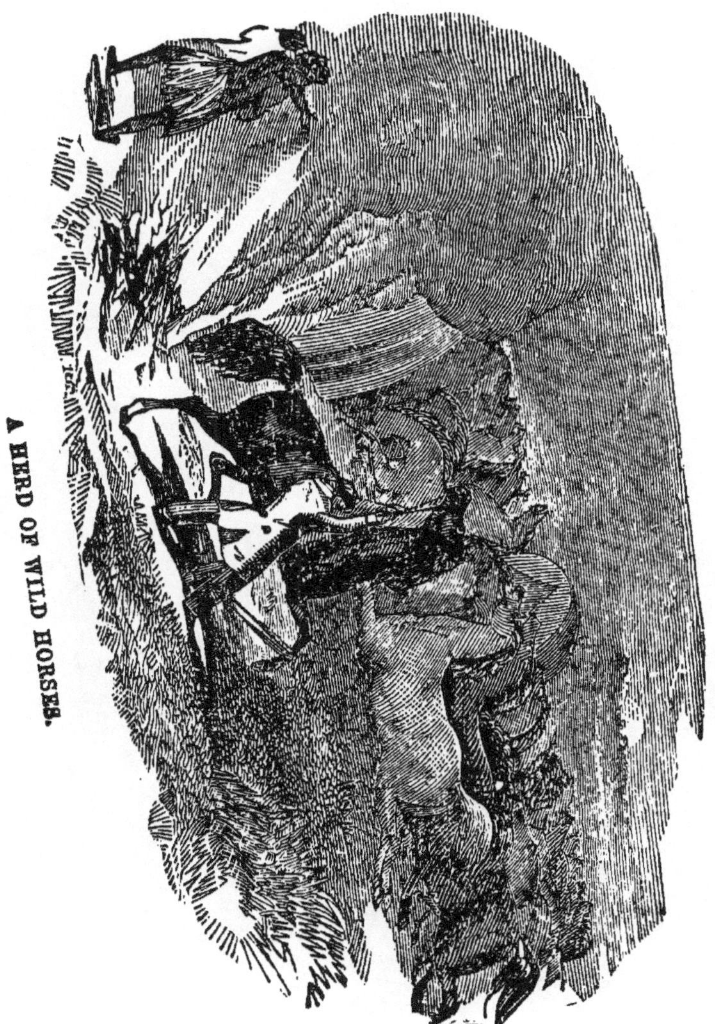

A HERD OF WILD HORSES.

going on, a parcel of mischievous boys had perched themselves on a pile of firewood close to the corral; and being each armed in his way, with a lasso made of a small strip of hide, or of whipcord, got the first chance to noose the animals as they rushed out. They seldom failed to throw successfully, but their slender cords broke like cobwebs. One wicked urchin, indeed, more bold than the rest, mounted himself on a donkey that happened to be on the spot; and taking the lasso which belonged to it—for no description of animal that is ever mounted is without this essential equipment — and placing himself so as not to be detected by the men, he threw it gallantly over the first bullock's neck. As soon as it became tight, away flew the astonished donkey and his rider: the terrified boy soon tumbled off; but poor Neddy was dragged along the ground, till a more efficient force was made to co-operate with his unavailing resistance.

The immense abundance of horses in South America cannot be more strongly exemplified than by the following account:

"I have still in my possession," says Mr. Robertson, "a contract which I made in Goya, with an estanciero, for twenty thousand wild horses, to be taken on his estate, at the price of a medio each; that is to say, three pence for each horse or mare! The slaughter of them cost three pence a head more; the staking and cleaning of the hides, once more, three pence; and lastly, a like sum for the carting to Goya: making the whole not one shilling for each skin. Of this contract ten thousand animals were delivered; the skins were packed in bales and sold in Buenos Ayres at six rials, or three shillings each, and they sold ultimately in England for seven or eight shillings, that is, for about twenty-eight or thirty times the first cost of the horse from which the skin was taken. Such is the accumulative value sometimes of the produce which is taken from the hands of the grower in one country before it gets into the hands of the consumer in another."

Hunting the Shetland Pony.

THE sheltie, or pony of the Shetland isles, is a very diminutive animal, sometimes not more than thirty inches high, and rarely exceedingly thirty-eight. He is often exceeding beautiful, with a small head, good tempered countenance, a short neck, fine toward the throttle, shoulders low and thick, in so little a creature far from being a ble-

(271)

mish—back short, quarters expanded and powerful, legs flat and fine, and pretty round feet. These ponies, possess immense strength for their size; will fatten upon almost any thing, and are perfectly docile. Mr. Youatt says that one of them, three feet in height, carried a man of twelve stone forty miles in one day.

Pony hunting used to be one of the favorite amusements of the Welsh farmers and peasantry a century and a half ago, and it has not even now fallen into disuse. The following story of one of these expeditions is related in the Cambrian Magazine.

A farmer, named Hugo Garonwy, lived in the neighborhood of Llewyn Georgie. Although he handled the small tilt plough, and other farming tools in their due season, yet the catching of the merlin, the fox, and the hare, were pursuits more congenial to his tastes; and the tumbles and thumps which he received, and from which no pony hunter was exempt, served but to attach him to the sport. Rugged, however, as were the Merioneddshire coast and its environs,

and abounding with precipices and morasses, the hunter sometimes experienced
worse mishaps, and so it happened with
Garonwy.

He set out one morning with his lasso
coiled round his waist, and attended by
two hardy dependents and their greyhounds.
The lasso was then familiar to the Welsh-
man, and as adroitly managed by him as
by any Gaucho on the plains of South
America. As the hunters climbed the
mountain's brow, the distant herd of ponies
took alarm—sometimes galloping onwards,
and then suddenly halting and wheeling
round, snorting as if in defiance of the intruders, and furiously pawing the ground.
Garonwy, with the assistance of his ser-
vants and his greyhounds, contrived to coop
them up in the corner of the hills, where
perpendicular rocks prevented their escape.

Already had he captured three of the
most beautiful little fellows in the world,
which he expected to sell for £4 or £5 each
at the next Bala fair, to him a considerable
sum, and amounting to a fourth of the an-

nual rent which he paid for his sheep walk. There remained, however, one most untameable creature, whose crested, mane and flowing tail, and wild eye, and distended nostril showed that he was a perfect Bucephalus of the hills; nor, indeed, was it safe to attack him in the ordinary way. Many of the three year olds had been known to break the legs of their pursuers, and some had been dismounted and trampled to death.

Garonwy was determined to give the noble fellow a chase over the hills, and so overcome him by fatigue before the lasso was flung. The dogs were unslipped, and off they went swift as the winds, Garonwy following, and the two assistants posted in a neighboring eminence. Vain was the effort to tire the merlin. Hugo, naturally impatient, and without waiting to ascertain that the coils were all clear, flung the lasso over the head of the wild horse. The extremity of the cord was twisted round his own body, and tightening as the animal struggled, the compression became insupportable, and at length, in spite of every effort to disengage himself, Garonwy was dragged from his horse.

The affrighted merlin, finding himself manacled by the rope, darted off with all the speed of which he was capable, dragging poor Garonwy over the rocky ground and stunted brushwood. This occurred at some distance from the men. They called in their dogs that the speed of the merlin might not be increased; but ere they could arrive at the spot at which the accident happened, the horse and the man had vanished. Whether the sufferings of the hunter were protracted, or he was dashed against a rock at the commencement of the horrible race, was never known; but the wild animal, frenzied and blinded by terror, rushed over a beetling cliff, at a considerable distance, overhanging the sea-shore, and the hunter and the horse were found at the bottom, a misshapen semblance of what they had been when living.

Adventure with a Python.

There is a species of snake called the python, which closely resembles the true boa, but is larger and more terrible. Pythons are found in India, Africa, and Australia. Wild hogs, antelopes, and even men fall victims to these monsters. They are not poisonous, but strangle and crush their large victims by powerful compression. The ular sawa, or great python of the Sunda Isles is said to exceed, when full grown, thirty feet in length. But the pythons of India have excited the most dread, by their awful depredations.

Some years ago, an Indian ship was passing near the Sunderlands, and the captain sent a boat into one of the creeks to obtain some fresh fruits. The inhabitants

(276)

ADVENTURE WITH A PYTHON.

24

of this inhospitable region are few and miserable. They have but little communication with the rest of the world, and that only occurs, when passing vessels send to purchase some of their fruits, which they are chiefly engaged in cultivating. Having reached the shore, the crew, six in number, moored the boat under a bank. A lascar was left to take care of it, while the rest of the party went after the fruit.

The day was very hot. Not a breath stirred the trees, whose branches overhung the water. The birds had sought the cool groves farther inland. The sky was without a cloud, and like burnished brass—the water its reflection. The air seemed standing still and panting for a cool breath. The lascar waited patiently. The party did not return. Probably, they were forced to proceed farther to get the fruit than they expected. A half-hour passed and they did not appear. The lascar, made listless by the intense heat, sank down under the seats of the boat, and gradually yielded to the soft soothings of sleep. In a few moments

after lying down, he was dead to all exter-
nal things.   He did not feel the heat.

Suddenly, the head—eager and dreadful—
of an enormous snake, of the python species, peered over the branch of a tree, near
the boat.   It quickly glanced around, as if
to assure itself that no wakeful foes were
near, and slowly stretched its head downward toward the boat.   Good heavens! the
lascar remains unconscious of the monster's
advance.   How it licks its slimy chops in
anticipation of a good meal! What length!
Many feet are stretched forward, and many
remain coiled around the trunks of the trees.
Its skin is glossy, variegated, and very
beautiful; but, oh! how deadly will be the
enormous folds!   It has reached the boat,
and has begun to coil itself around the body
of the sleeping lascar.   Its jaws, foul and
slimy, are extended; its forked tongue pro-
trudes.   Soon the coil will crush the bones
of the man.   A yell of fear and surprise
pierces the air.   The lascar awakes to feel
his awful situation, and to know that his
friends have arrived, and are at work for

deliverance. A portion of the monster's tail is severed with a hatchet, and he lost the power of doing mischief. The poor lascar shrieks to his companions to save him.

A few more blows with oars and hatchets and the serpent is despatched, its head being severed and thrown into the water. The lascar is rescued, and is but slightly bruised. Filled with joy and gratitude he embraces his preservers. Upon measurement, this serpent was found to be sixty-two feet and some inches in length. With the skin and some of the fat, which the natives esteem for its curative properties, and the fruit which they had purchased, the crew of the boat returned to the ship.

24*

Capture of Giraffes.

THE Zoological Society having made known its wish to possess living specimens of the giraffe, the task of procuring them was undertaken by M. Thibaut, who, having had twelve years' experience in African travel, was well qualified for the arduous pursuit.

M. Thibaut quitted Cairo in April, 1834, and after sailing up the Nile as far as Wadi

HUNTING THE GIRAFFE.

Halfa, the second cataract, took camels and proceeded to Debbat, a province of Dongolah, whence he started for the Desert of Kordofan. Being perfectly acquainted with the locality, and on friendly terms with the Arabs, he attached them still more by the desire of profit; all were desirous of accompanying him in pursuit of the giraffes, for up to that time, they had hunted them solely for the sake of the flesh, which they ate, and the skin, of which they made bucklers and sandals. The party proceeded to the south-west of Kordofan, and in August were rewarded by the sight of two beautiful giraffes; a rapid chase of three hours, on horses accustomed to the fatigues of the desert, put them in possession of the largest of these noble animals; unable to take her alive, the Arabs killed her with blows of the sabre, and cutting her to pieces, carried the meat to their head-quarters, which had been established in a wooded situation, an arrangement necessary for their own comfort, and to secure pasturage for their camels. They deferred till the following day the motherless young one, which the Arabs knew they would have no difficulty in again discovering. The Arabs quickly covered the live embers with slices of the meat, which M. Thibaut pronounced to be excellent.

On the following morning the party started at daybreak in search of the young giraffe, of which they had lost sight not far from the camp. The sandy desert is well adapted to afford indications to a hunter, and in a very short time they were on the track of the object of their pursuit: they followed the traces with rapidity and in silence, lest the creature should be alarmed while yet at a distance; but after a laborious chase of several hours through brambles and thorny trees, they at last succeeded in capturing the coveted prize.

It was now necessary to rest for three or four days, in order to render the giraffe sufficiently tame, during which period an Arab constantly held it at the end of a long cord; by degrees it became accustomed to the presence of man, and was induced to

take nourishment, but it was found necessary to insert a finger into its mouth to deceive it into the idea that it was with its
dam; it then sucked freely. When captured, its age was about nineteen months.
Five giraffes were taken by the party, but
the cold weather of December, 1834, killed
four of them in the desert, on the route to
Dongolah; happily that first taken survived,
and reached Dongolah in January, 1835,
after a sojourn of twenty-two days in the
desert.

Unwilling to leave with a solitary speci-
men, M. Thibaut returned to the desert,
where he remained three months, crossing it
in all directions, and frequently exposed to
great hardships and privations; but he was
eventually rewarded by obtaining three giraffes, all smaller than the first. A great
trial awaited them, as they had to proceed
by water the whole distance from Wadi
Hafa to Cairo, and thence to Alexandria
and Malta, besides the voyage to England.
They suffered considerably at sea during a
passage of twenty-four days in very tem-

pestuous weather, and on reaching Malta, in November, were detained in quarantine twenty-five days more; but despite of all these difficulties, they reached England in safety, and on the 25th of May were conducted to the Gardens.

At daybreak, the keepers and several gentlemen of scientific distinction arrived at the Brunswick wharf, and the animals were handed over to them. The distance to the Gardens was not less than six miles, and some curiosity, not unmingled with anxiety, was felt as to how this would be accomplished. Each giraffe was led between two keepers, by means of long reins attached to the head; the animals walked at a rapid pace, generally in advance of their conductors, but were perfectly tractable. It being so early in the morning, few persons were about, but the astonishment of those who did behold the unlooked-for procession, was ludicrous in the extreme. As the giraffes stalked by, followed by M. Thibaut and others, in Eastern costume, the worthy policemen and early coffee-sellers

stared with amazement, and a few revellers,
whose reeling steps proclaimed their dissi-
pation, evidently doubted whether the singular figures they beheld were real flesh
and bone, or fictions conjured up by their
potations; their gaze of stupid wonder indicating that of the two they inclined to the
latter opinion.

When the giraffes entered the park, and
first caught sight of the green trees, they
became excited, and hauled upon the reins,
waving the head and neck from side to side,
with an occasional caracole and kick out of
the hind legs, but M. Thibaut contrived to
coax them along with pieces of sugar, of
which they were very fond, and he had the
satisfaction of depositing his valuable
charges, without accident or misadventure,
in the sanded paddock prepared for their
reception.

A Brush with a Bison.

BY JOHN MILLS, ESQ.

PREVIOUSLY to the introduction of Birmingham and Sheffield manufactures into the Indian market, the weapons used in war and hunting were of an exceedingly primitive kind. Instead of rifles, scalping knives, tomahawks, and two-edged lances of polished steel, the North American brave possessed but a short bow made of bone with

(290)

TRADING WITH THE INDIANS.

twisted sinews for strings, and a quiver of flint-tipped arrows, with a stone hatchet, comprised his whole stand-of-arms. As a matter of course, the more destructive kinds of instruments introduced at once increased the slaughter of game, and from the eagerness of the traders to exchange their goods for skins, led the Indians to destroy those animals by wholesale which formerly were killed only for food and clothing for themselves. Even at certain seasons of the year, when the fur of the buffalo is in the worst possible condition, it has been known for vast herds to be exterminated merely for their tongues, which would be bartered for a few gallons of villainous whisky.

The numbers still raging over the prairies are, doubtless, very great, extending from the western frontier to the western verge of the Rocky Mountains, and from the 30th to the 55th degree of northern latitude; but, as if the end was fixed for the extermination of this the principal provision of the Indian, with the Indian himself, they are rapidly becoming thinned, and in a few years it is highly probable that a buffalo, in its native state, will be a rare animal on the American continent.

It is worthy of a passing reflection to glance at the particular purposes for which the buffalo was assigned: to supply the three chief wants of the Indian, as they are those of the white man—food, raiment, and lodging. The flesh affords ample provision, the skin robes for clothing, bedding, and covering to his wigwam, while, as a further utility, the hoofs are melted into a glue to assist him in fabricating his shield, arrows, and other necessary articles for savage life. It may, therefore be imagined that the buffalo is indispensable to the Indian's simple existence; for whatever may have been said and written concerning schemes for his civilization, I am quite certain that, from his innate indolence, love of roving, fierce passions, and unconquerable desire for the excitement of war and hunting, nothing can be more impossible than that any such attempts should meet with a different result than positive defeat.

We were now on the verge of the upper prairies, no longer enameled with flowers and flowering plants, but covered with a short, coarse herbage, called "buffalo grass," on which the buffalo loves to feed. These hunting grounds are far easier to ride over, from being free of vines and entangling shrubs which interlace each other in impenetrable masses, although the yawning clefts, made by the water courses, the wallows caused by the buffaloes forming baths for themselves by ripping the earth open with their heads in soft, oozy spots, and the burrowing of that sharp and watchful little animal the prairie dog, cause both horse and horseman to run considerable risk when taking a spin over the flat.

The serious object of the expedition was now on the eve of being realized, and the land of promise being gained, every preparation had been made the succeeding morning for a regular buffalo hunt. In addition to my rifle and pistols, I carried a long lance with the shaft made of the toughest ash. This weapon I found rather unwieldy and awkward, and saw how different it looked in the hands of my companions; but Hawkeye insisted that it was indispensable, as I could not attempt the use of the bow and arrow.

Stripped of all superfluous garments, and fully equipped for the expedition, my companions mounted their horses, with their lassos uncoiled and trailing upon the ground, as invariably is the rule in war or hunting, for the purpose of facilitating the re-capture of the animal should an unlucky separation take place between the rider and his saddle. In an extended line, or by the familiar description of Indian file, we began this march as usual just at ruddy daybreak, and were not far advanced on the great prairie stretching before us like a vast and limitless ocean, when Blackwolf, who headed the force, reined in his dark iron-grey steed with a sudden jerk which sent him nearly upon his haunches. In an instant all was commotion. Arrows were drawn from their quivers, bow-strings tried and thrummed, lances poised, and every eye directed to the

BLACKWOLF.

spot on which the chief fixed his earnest and flashing gaze.

Not two miles distant, and grazing in fancied security on a piece of table land as level as a bowling-green, a large herd of buffalo was descried, looking at the distance like so many black specks on the waste. Some I could perceive were lying down, and the scene altogether may be compared, without violence to the imagination, to what the tourist may witness by the aid of rail-roads, within a few hours of the metropolis, in a canter across Dartmoor or Exmouth, and where no dread exists of Pawnees and Camanches.

It was decided that we should head the herd, and endeavor to drive them back towards the encampment, in order to save as little time and trouble as possible in getting the meat and skins to that quarter. In prosecuting this scheme we had to make a wide circle from the direct course, and, indeed, it would have been impossible to approach them in any other way, as we were down the wind, and their powers of scent, like those given to the denizens of the wild in general, are of the most acute order.

"You know, major," observed Hawkeye, as he turned our horses considerably to the left, for the purpose of covering our circumventing manœuvre under the screen of two lines of bluffs running parallel with each other, "You know, major," repeated he, with a sly twinkle of satire in his snake-like eyes, "for all Britishers dat come here say *you know* to every thing, dat buff*alo* smell Indian mile off. No see far; but smell— Hah! no saying how far buff*alo* smell."

It was a moment of the most thrilling excitement of my life, as with a swoop the Indians dashed ahead, and with halter and rein dangling free, to see their horses strain their utmost powers to outstrip the fugitives, and bring them within the reach of bow and lance. Nigger, I may confidently state, did his best, although in a very short distance, it was conclusively obvious that he could not long live the pace we were going at. The pony, however, rattled away with his ears thrown back like a racehorse, at his final effort, and we were within a few score yards at the moment of Blackwolf's bearing close to the right side of the nearest buffalo, and drawing his bow at the moment of passing, buried the arrow to the feather. In an instant the horse wheeled to avoid the thrust which the wounded buffalo often makes; but Blackwolf's victim was stricken in a vital part, and he rolled over struggling and bleeding in the throes of deadly agony. Right and left the Indians scoured the plain in hot pursuit of the doomed and frightened animals, and never halting in the chase, but rushing from one to another as the huge beasts shouldered along in their ungainly gallop down the valleys and over the bluffs, and across huge gaping rents in the prairie, caused by the winter torrents, brought them to the ground like skittles from well-directed hands.

There appeared to be no chance for me to flesh my maiden lance, and I began to despair of adding a single head to the number slain, when I caught sight of a solitary fugitive stealing away through a stony ravine much to the left of the line which the rest had taken, and from his action I concluded that he had met with a wound which materially interfered with his speed. With an unequivocal disposition to refuse taking any other course than the one he was pursuing, Nigger began to wrestle for the mastership, and being encumbered with my lance, I had some little difficulty in pricking him toward the point where the buffalo, alone in his flight, was using his best energies to escape. The pointed iron, however, prevailed, and the plucky little horse, seeing the animal scramble over a conical shaped hillock in the distance, settled himself again in his best pace, and carried me forward in winning style.

After floundering through a spongy bottom, in which were several wallows of some dozen feet in diameter made by the buffaloes, I found myself near enough to try the the effect of lead, and dropping my lance to trail along the ground by a thong attached to my wrist, for I was not expert enough to handle both it and my rifle, as an Indian

would have done without inconvenience, 1
brought the barrels to bear and gave the
contents of both just as Nigger's nose was
on a level with the haunch of one of the
largest and blackest bulls that ever ranged
over a western plain.

With due regard for the preservation of
himself, and possibly his rider, Nigger made
an abrupt curve, and sheering off, almost
at a right angle, avoiding an ugly, vicious
thrust, which the bull might have made
much more effective than my brace of bullets, had not the sagacity of the pony taught
him to avoid it.   Upon reining in my gallant and discreet little steed, and turning
his head again toward the buffalo, I saw
that he was standing still, and giving as
bold a front as was ever offered to an enemy.
Coming to a corresponding attitude, I deliberately reloaded my rifle, and approached
him with the greatest caution; for whether
he intended to await my second attack, or
plunge forward and send me and Nigger
skimming to some unknown corner of the
earth, appearing a matter of doubt not quite

made up. After a few brief moments for reconnoitring, I urged Nigger to advance to within less than thirty paces of where the bull stood glaring at us, with his curling mane and beard sweeping below his knees, and his distended jaws dropping foam, scarlet dyed with blood. Nothing, indeed, can be imagined more ferocious than the wounded animal looked, fixing the peculiar white ball and black iris of his eyes upon us, under his shaggy frontlet, with the expression of the devil in a mood far from funny. Thinking it expedient to bring the contest to a conclusion without further waste of time, I essayed a manœuvre in order to obtain a sight of a more vulnerable part of my victim's carcass than that which, as I had been given to understand by Hawkeye, his head presented.

But, as the baited grimalkin turns to the worrying cur, so did the bull turn exactly with my movements, ever presenting his head, and nothing but his head. This proving exceedingly wearisome, and quickly exhausting the slender stock of patience with

A BUFFALO HUNT.

which nature supplied me at my birth, I resolved to try what a shot would do in the centre of his forehead, and steadying Nigger for a moment, snapped my left barrel at him, when with the crack down he dropped, and spurring forward in the belief that I had given him his *coup de grace*, I was not a little surprised to see him stagger again to his feet, ready to receive me on his two short black horns, curved in the best possible shape for the ripping business.

Perceiving, however, that notwithstanding that the last bullet had only flattened on his *os frontis*, he was fast sinking from the internal hemorrhage caused by the two first, which brought him to a check, I determined to expend no more valuable ammunition upon him, but inflict a final thrust or two of cold steel. Reslinging my rifle across my shoulders, I for the first time couched a lance for a deadly object, and rode at the bull's flank; but he was too quick for me, and turned as if upon a pivot. Round and round we went, Nigger, with pricked ears and nimble limbs, keeping a steady look upon the buffalo's movements, and far from liking the loud snorts of mingled rage and pain which he momentarily sent forth as we whirled about him. But the attempts of the enemy to foil our purpose grew gradually weaker, and at length, failing to twist with his former adroitness, I plunged the head of the lance to the shaft in his body, and as I plucked it out, the crimson current of his life poured forth, and falling upon his knees, he rolled over dead without a struggle.